CHRIS LOWRY

Flyover Zombie – a Post Apocalyptic Action Thriller

Contents

Thank you for taking the time to read. If you enjoyed it,...

1

FLYOVER ZOMBIE

No one knows how it started. Or if they do, they're not saying. The Fed's were building a wall at the Mexico border when it happened. Some smart bureaucrat shifted the resources over to California and moved the construction to the foothills of the Rocky Mountains.

It took eight days for a million workers to erect a fifteen-foot barrier and eight more to double it the entire length of the state.

They carried the steel plates up into the mountains and blocked off the middle.

A second wall went up along the Appalachian Trail. They were able to contain the outbreak in the middle.

Chicago was gone.

Canada had to fend for itself and the same for Mexico.

But the good old USA had the East, parts of the West and nothing in-between.

Nothing living anyway.
There were plenty of the dead.
1

LOS ANGELES –

"Have you heard from New York this morning?"
"DC protocol," the tech answered.

His job was simple. Monitor communications from the East, and surviving cities in California for indications of an outbreak.

A multichannel processor routed through airwave bands by the thousands, searching for chatter on cell phone traffic, radio broadcasts, and even CB radio lines. His role was to listen to the chatter and define anomalies.

Plus, do a daily check in with DC, NYC, and other major metro areas.

The daily check in served two purposes.

First, to reassure the people across the country that other survivors were still there after the dark of the night.

Second, to insure the survivors were following standard operating procedures in regards to staying healthy and alive.

"Go grab some shut eye," the supervisor patted him on the back.

Del Waters, the radio tech stood up from his station and stretched. Even then he kept his eyes on the blinking lights as they raced across the boards, blinking red and yellow until they hit on a channel.

Fast fingers were required to click on the green, so they could listen in, adjust the feed and monitor if needed.

His replacement, Bobby Shannon slid into the seat he vacated and went eyes up on the board.

Assured, Del slapped his shoulder and stepped away.

He wasn't sure how many times he blinked through the night, but his eyeballs felt like gritty balls of sand. No matter the count, it wasn't enough.

But they made it through a night without incident, which was a mark in the W column.

Incidents were always bad.

Three nights ago, LAPD responded to a domestic disturbance call. Turned out to be a fight where the woman stabbed her abusive husband, and didn't call for a body disposal unit because she didn't want to get in trouble.

At least that's what they pieced together.

They were both zombie by the time police arrived, and LA lost one of its boys in blue to a bite on the arm before others were able to put both Z down with headshots.

The Council had a rule.

Bring out your dead. Stab them in the head.

"Do you want to grab a cup of coffee?"

Del turned from his stretch and watched Jeri fight back a yawn with the back of her hand.

They had been working side by side since the advent of the virus, and he wanted to ask her out someday.

At first, he wasn't sure they would live that long, and even though he wanted to grab life by the throat and drink the nectar, it was more fun to live with the thought and ignore the action.

Jeri had been a student at UCLA.

Like most people who did not have specific skillset jobs, she was recruited to monitor the wall, monitor the drones, monitor the radio channels.

Just like Del.

If George Orwell envisioned 1984 with Zombies, this would be the world they lived in.

But they were safe.

"It will just keep me up," he couldn't bring himself to look into her perfect brown eyes.

And alive.

"Say yes, you fool," he screamed at himself.
     The little voice inside his head pushing him to be brave. "She asked you out."

"Some other time then?"

She sounded hopeful.
     Or did he imagine that.

"Sure."

"Help, please!"

Bobby Shannon clicked on the blinking green button to bring a young girl's voice up full.

"Please God, help me."

Shannon typed in a command code to record the audio, and sent a signal to the satellite to triangulate the position of the call.

"It's outside the wall," he called over his shoulder.

Del, Jeri and the supervisor moved to behind his chair. Del fought the urge to start issuing orders, since Bobby looked like he knew what he was doing.

Already a message was being sent to the Council, per SOP. Survivors outside rated their attention.

At the same time, more messages were sent off to DC and NYC.

Information inside the flyover zone was hard to come by, and meticulously documented when they did.

"This is Council Command," the supervisor lifted his headset and keyed into the channel. "Where are you?"

"I don't know," she sobbed across the speaker. "Our plane went down."

"Plane?" his eyebrow shot up as he glanced at Del.

No planes had been allowed to fly since the first outbreak was contained. Air travel spread the contagion too fast.

"We were coming from New York. Help me, please."

"Miss," said the supervisor. "Did you crash? Are you injured?"

"We had to land," she said. "The pilot died, and we went down somewhere. On a road."

"Got it," Bobby announced and pulled up an image on the computer screen. "Kansas."

"Are you in a secure location?"

"We locked the pilot in the cockpit. We can hear him in there. He's one of them."

"Miss," the supervisor scribbled instructions to Del and handed it to him. "Who are you? I'm letting the Council know your situation, but we need more information."

Del glanced at the note. It said, Get Ballantine.

"Tell my Dad," she sobbed.

"Who is your father?"

"He's Roger Ballantine."

Then she screamed and the radio went silent.

2

2

Roger Ballantine was not a man used to hearing the word no.

There were people who thought politicians ran the world, but Ballantine could explain to you with a veneer capped smile that money ran the world, and he who had the money was King.
  It had always been so.

He was King of New York when he ran real estate deals that inflated property values into the billions, and he got out before that bubble burst.

He did the same in Los Angeles racking up another billion before it collapsed too.

He took government bailout money and used it to buy a Television Network, which made thirty-three billion dollars a year before the Zombie outbreak.

Ballantine was immensely impressed that he got his company a tax refund of over two hundred million dollars while making so much profit.

"Mr. Ballantine," his assistant stood in the doorway to his penthouse office.

Her boss didn't bother to look up from his expansive desk. It was the only piece of furniture in the office except for his plush leather chair.

The décor was a choice in minimalism, and an effort on Ballantine's part to show that even though space was at a premium, he had a thousand square feet just for his desk.

"What?" he barked.

"The Council is calling a quorum."

He didn't put down his pen even though he wasn't working on anything of importance at the moment.

Since the fall and the construction of the wall, the Council had voted to stop using television for entertainment and make it news and education twenty-four seven.

The news was about the safety and rebuilding efforts. The education was how to.

How to grow food.

How to filter rainwater.

How to compost waste, how to survive.

It was disgusting, he thought.

But at least he was in charge of it.

In charge of it all, and even if he had been voted down the first two times he brought it up, his associates had discovered a couple of pressure points he could push on a few members and the third time the vote would go his way.

He'd bring back entertainment to coddle the masses and take their minds off the flyover states.

He set the pen down in and coiled out of his seat.

The buttons on his Armani were made from ivory and he slipped the top two through the holes in his coat and brushed off imaginary lint.

Ballantine knew people respected authority with style and he wasn't about to let the end of the world take that control from him.

"Take notes," he snapped as he stepped past her.

She was new and he hadn't bothered to learn her name.

His last assistant jumped off the roof of the building after a Council meeting where they learned a suburb of Denver had fallen.

One of the members said that was her hometown.

The one before that turned Z after being bitten.

It just didn't pay to waste time learning about them if they were going to die.

He marched down the hallway and took the stairs down eighteen flights to the Council chamber.

He hated every step.

Normally, he would use the stairs to keep trim, but since the Council voted to restrict electrical use to essentials, they forced him to use them, and that pissed him off.

He heard the clatter of sensible shoes on the steps behind him.

"Good girl," he muttered.

This one was good at taking orders.

He liked that.

Ballantine was a man who liked to give orders.

3

3

"Listen up," Captain Seamus Sharp stepped through the door to the ready room and eyeballed his platoon. There were two fire teams in the room, twelve men comprised of six man squads.

They jumped to their feet and snapped to attention.

"Good," he thought to himself. "Old timers were teaching the new meat."

He moved to the front of the room and wished for a laptop. He knew it was a crutch from the before days, when mission briefings were conducted using PowerPoint presentations. But it was the way he had trained.

Now he had an overhead with a weak 30-watt lightbulb, which the men could barely see on a dust colored screen.

The new meat was the result of the death of a lot of old meat.

The Army took the brunt of the zombie assault during the initial outbreak.
  "That's not true," he muttered as he turned to face the men.

The Marines were the ones who took it on the chin. Ten thousand men in Camp Pendleton turned loose to wreak hell on the zombies.

They camped on the outer edges of the town to enforce the just declared martial law, and the Z virus swept their encampment.

In twelve hours, they lost ninety percent of the fighting force because no one was sure what they were dealing with and the Marines didn't fire on each other.

The Army didn't fare much better.

Ft Irwin sent out tanks to man the borders, especially along Mexico and TJ to prevent an onslaught of Mexican Z from crossing.

"We've got new orders," he told his men.

Five of them were conscripted from the streets of LA. Zero combat experience, little more than basic training in the National Guard, and even then, their military occupations were support services.

He needed killers and he got quartermasters.

"The HMFIC has declared from up on high that you are going for a plane ride."

Their eyeballs swiveled on him hard, the weight of the stares making him wish for the laptop even more.

Few planes had been up since the virus started.

Those carried VIP government officials and dignitaries from other countries, if the scuttlebutt was true.

But no soldiers had been flown in almost a year.

"At 0300 today, a civilian craft went down in Kansas. It was a forced landing, not a crash. There was radio contact made with the survivors. Chairman Ballantine has declared a rescue operation and we are the lucky sons of bitches who get to go get them."

He let them mutter then.

No one in the room had pulled wall duty either, but they knew what was on the other side.

But they had no idea what was left in the middle.
   "Is this a Suicide Squad thing?" one of his men asked.

He was regular military, a giant of a man that somehow got the original name Bear from his DI and it stuck. It could have been his grizzly disposition or a bastardization of his surname, Barrington.

Either way the giant was from Sharp's original squad, a combat survivor from the street clean ups in Compton and Long Beach.

"I think you mean Force 10 or something," Javier nudged him.

Where Bear was tall and wide, Javi was rail thin and average.

"Mutt and Jeff," Sharp interrupted them.

"Save that Roger and Ebert shit for downtime."

"Who are Roger and Ebert?" Bear asked.

"Who are Mutt and Jeff?" Javi added.

A couple of fucking comedians.

He'd have to say something in private to them. He didn't want the new guys getting any ideas about the way he ran a meeting.

But these two had saved his life a dozen times over, maybe more.
    They could play at being funny if they wanted.

"This is not a kamikaze mission," he smirked in their general direction and earned a grin of his own.

"Nobody dies. Nobody gets hurt. We parachute in so we don't attract Z attention. Find the plane. Find the survivors. Call for extract."

"Too easy," said Bear.

"Sounds like it. Our LZ is tight. We know there is Z activity in the area because of the radio contact. And we're flying in blind."

One of several consequences of the zombie virus was how quickly they lost communications across the country.

It was a complication of domino errors. A tech turned Z wrecked keyboards or sent satellites into decaying orbits. Backup systems got overloaded. The center could not hold.

Sharp didn't know the specifics of each break down, but he had to live with the results of it.

They couldn't pull a satellite over the affected area to gather intelligence, so they were working with World War II type technology, at least when it came to that.

He looked at his Rolex Submariner watch, a relic of a bygone era that still worked.

"Kit up," he ordered. "We travel ammo heavy in one hour."

"Loaded for Bear?" Javi nudged his companion.

"Like a Pope in the woods," Bear answered.

"Man, that don't make any sense."

Sharp left them to their ribbing and to get their gear together.

He had his go bag ready, so sliding into the Kevlar vest and armor units would only take twenty minutes. He wanted to spend the rest of the time trying to find a map of where they were going.

4

Pam Ballantine opened her eyes and stared at the ceiling. She popped out of the bed, nearly collapsed on the floor and tried not to scream.

A strange looking man stood by the door and watched her.

"Where am I?" she croaked.

Her hands ran across the simple nightgown she wore and she realized she wasn't wearing panties or a bra. It pissed her off.

"Who took my clothes?"

The man held up both hands in a universal sign of surrender.

"No one hurt you," he explained. "No one touched you."

"No one is going to hurt me," she snarled. "Where are my clothes?"

Then she realized she was in the room alone. Simple, four white walls, no windows, just the wooden door, and the bed she had been on.

No closet to hide her clothes. No other doors to the room.

And none of the people who had been on the plane with her.

"I'll have your clothes brought," said her captor.

He reached behind him and pulled the door open to step through.

Pam watched him shut it, then padded across the cold tile floor in her bare feet and tried the knob.

It wasn't locked.

She opened the door and peeked out.

The man was walking down a short corridor, past several other numbered doors just like hers.

Pam moved into the hallway and opened a second door.

One of the people from the plane was lying in the bed, wrists and feet tied to the metal posts with straps.

Who the hell had them?

She moved into the shadowy room and started untying the survivor.

"Don't worry," she whispered. "I'm going to help you get out of here."

She couldn't remember the woman's name, and maybe hadn't even been introduced to her.

The truth was she hadn't been paying much attention to anyone on the plane, the novelty of flying out to Los Angeles occupied a big part of her mind.

She was focused on her father, the strings he pulled to get her out of New York and to him in LA.

She had worked through his connections in the City to help him on Council business and instead of giving her a seat representing NYC, he recalled her to him.

She remembered this woman was reading a book though, which in itself wasn't a novelty, but it was a copy of a novel she had wanted to read before the fall.

Pam had made a note to ask about borrowing it when they landed, or finding a way to get it once they were settled into their west coast homes.

The woman grunted and strained at the straps.

It made it harder to untie the knots.

"Hold on," Pam soothed her. "I'll have you free in a minute."

She finished the knot on her left wrist and reached across her for the right.

The woman grabbed the back of her hair and yanked Pam down.

She buried her face in her neck hard, and Pam squealed, struggling to get her hands where she could push off the bed.

The woman had something in her mouth, a ball gag or rubber ball and it ground into the flesh in Pam's neck.

"Stop!" Pam shouted.

She finally smacked the woman with the heel of her palm, and when that didn't work, slugged her with a closed fist.

The ball knocked loose from her mouth and bounced across the floor, but the woman let her go and Pam backed away.

Her eyes adjusted to the darkness and she bit back a scream.

The woman had gone Z.

That's why they strapped her to the bed, why they gagged her.

Now she was ripping at the restraint on her other arm, growling and moaning to reach Pam.

She got her arm free, couldn't stand so dragged her torso out of the bed and onto the floor.

Her tied legs scraped the bed after her, bending at the unnatural angle until they both snapped with a loud crack.

Pam stifled another scream and ran through the doorway.

She bounced off the thick white uniform of her captor and fell back into the room.

This time, she didn't try to stop the scream as the Z edged closer, dragging the bed with her.

A tall black man pushed past the white-haired man, pulled a pistol from a shoulder holster and shot the zombie.

The echo of the bullet off the wall receded, and all Pam could hear was the rushing beat of her heart in her ears.

The tall man holstered his pistol.

"Did she bite you?"

Pam shook her head.

"Are you bit?" he asked again.

"No," she shuddered. "No, I'm not."

She composed herself, taking a deep breath and pushed off the floor to stand in front of him.

"Why have you taken me prisoner?"

The black man snorted.

"Lady, this isn't a prison. It's a hospital. We saved your life. Twice."

She stared at him as he let it sink in.

The white-haired man muttered in his shoulder and held out a sack of clothes.

"It looks like we're going to save it again. Get dressed."

5

5

Sharp had been out of a plane one hundred and thirty-seven times and hated every jump.

He hated all the old jokes about abandoning a perfectly good aircraft and never bought into the cult of thought about death from above.

He knew he was safe.

He knew the odds of landing well, and injury.

He also was particularly adept at jumping.

He didn't like it.

The adrenaline rush was not his drug of choice.

He liked things calm, cool and steady.

And he would have preferred it if they were jumping in daylight into an area he was familiar with.

A night jump into hostile territory left him with an acid gurgle in his stomach.

Even after he exited the rear of the cargo plane, number three of twelve out the door in four seconds, and his chute popped, he studied the dark terrain below, trying to make out features, topography, any landmarks he could remember.

There were no lights below.

He had seen a picture of the United States taken from the International Space Station once, the East and West Coast lit up like Christmas trees, and only small splotches of light through the middle.

Now there was nothing in the zombie infested wasteland.

The streetlights were gone.

The porchlights were gone.

There was only darkness, and he had to rely on the glowing numbers on his altimeter to tell him to flare.

Then he could see a darker patch below and he could tell he was close.

He flared again, pulling on the cords attached to the sides of his chute that arrested his descent, and started running his feet.

He knew to hit and roll with it in the dark, and when he felt the ground under his feet, did just that.

The chute collapsed behind him and he was up, stripping out of the harness and checking his gear.

All good.

He clicked the safety off his rifle, adjusted the strap across his chest and listened for the sound of the other men landing.

George "Georgie" Pie stood up from his landing and clicked a red light over his head to signal the others to a rally point.

Sharp took off across the field toward the red light.

He heard the Z before he saw them.

Who knows what drew them to the field. A butterfly, a badger, or maybe just a plastic sack swishing in the wind.

No matter, it sounded like more than one so he froze, readied his weapon, and tried to triangulate on the sound.

He heard a canopy flutter above his head, and a pair of boots smacked him across the temple and knocked him flat.

Sharp fumbled to his knees, and heard one of his men land in the small herd of Z. He couldn't tell who.

The man screamed, a boyish yelp of pain and surprise and then it escalated into a high-pitched wail of agony.

Sharp lifted his rifle and opened fire.

Flames licked the end of his barrel as he sprayed the shadowy figures of the herd.

His men zeroed in on his position and added their bullets to his own.

It was over in seconds.

"Medic," Sharp commanded and shuffled through the grass toward the decimated herd.

He listened to Doc fall in step behind him.

The man's name was Rodriguez, but every medic in the Army was always called Doc.

Sharp tried to call him Bones once as a salute to Star Trek, but no one else in the squad was a sci fi fan, so he stuck with Doc.

The Z were dead. Most of them.

"Georgie, knife," Sharp ordered.

Georgie slung his weapon and pulled a long black KBAR from a sheath on his vest. He dispatched the remaining zombies with swift thrusts into the head.

"Doc?"

Doc shook his head.

Sharp leaned down over his man, and ignored the hash of his legs below the knees and waist.

"Two Way," he said.

One of the new guys, a National Guardsman who was their radio operator.

The man had taken friendly fire too, which was a kick in the nuts, but he was dead now. Nothing to be done.

Besides, the Z bite was fatal from the moment he landed.

Georgie kneeled to knife him.

"I got it," said Sharp.

He did the hard part himself on this man.

"Damn it," Georgie rolled the body over after
    Sharp stabbed him.

He shined his flashlight onto the communications array

strapped to the man's back. It was shot all to hell.

"Salvaged?" Sharp asked.

Georgie shrugged and unfastened it.

The radio came off in three pieces.

"I'm no Com Tech," said Georgie. "But I think it's toast."

Bear and Javi moved in closer.

"Bear thinks we can use the radio from the plane."

Sharp nodded.

"Good thinking. Round 'em up Sergeant."

Georgie got the rest of the squad in line and Sharp moved them out in the direction of the road and where the plane was supposed to be.

6

6

Ballantine stood at the center of the communications station and glared.

He glared at the blinking lights, glared at the back of the communication tech's heads, glared at the man in charge of the group.

The Com Techs could ignore him, but the supervisor shrank under his gaze and looked around for a way to escape.

The man sent up a silent prayer for one of the buttons to flash green, anything that he could use as an excuse to leave the room.

"They should have landed by now."

The pilot updated them on when the squad had parachuted in three minutes ago.

Ballantine gave them extra time to land and assess, but now they were overdue for a check in.

The man next to him huffed.

It irritated the shit out of Ballantine.

"You just wasted a good team for one person."

Ballantine ignored him.

"I voted against this. I told the Council that you were out of your mind. We don't do rescue missions, not anymore."

The man huffed again.

Ballantine looked at the stars on his chevrons and wondered how the hell the man had risen so far in rank without a spine.

"They had to dig pretty far down the fucking barrel to move you up, didn't they General?"

"Excuse me?"

"I understand we are short manned, but Jesus, what were you before? In the accounting department?"

"I earned my rank," the General puffed out his chest and shook the medals on his lapel.

"I bet you fucking did," Ballantine said.

"I wouldn't have ordered this to save one person."

"It's not one person, it's– how many people are in the group?" he snarled at his assistant.

"Nine," she whispered.

"Speak up damn it."

"Nine," she answered and if it wasn't louder, it was an octave higher and he could make out the word.

"There you have it. See, we're saving nine citizens."

"You sent in my men to save nine people."

"Don't be ridiculous General. I sent in your men to save my daughter. I don't give a fuck if they save anyone else."

"One human life."

Ballantine could see the man was going to be a problem.

He had enough problems. Maybe it was time to retire the General.

"We've already lost so many," he said. "And this is my little girl."

"On an unauthorized flight."

"I authorized it."

"DC didn't. New York didn't. What if one of them is infected."

Ballantine walked away from the others and motioned the General to follow. He pitched his voice low so he couldn't be overheard.

"We're all infected General. If I killed you right now, you'd turn into a zombie and I'd slip this knife into your eyeball to pop your brain."

He put a hand on the long slim knife he carried on his waist.

"I'd like to see you try."

The Council chairman held up both hands.

"Did you think that was a threat?" he laughed.

The General flushed, a crimson stain creeping up from his neck to the tips of his ears.

"I don't make threats General," said Ballantine. "I take actions. While you were in some hut whining, and waiting for orders from the Pentagon, I sent crews into the desert to build our wall. I organized the police response. When the Governor called a committee meeting to wait it out, I called up the National Guard and saved millions of people. I am the reason you are standing in this room and not some walking dead piece of rotting shit."

Ballantine leaned close and glared down at the gray-haired man in front of him.

"I made it happen. All of it. You know this. It's information you've known for months. I don't ever make threats. I solve problems."

He bumped his forehead against the General's and forced him to back up.

The headbutt was light, just strong enough to leave a small red mark on each of their skin where they made contact.

Ballantine waited, eyes flashing, daring the General to fight back.

He didn't.

He bowed his head instead, a small nod of surrender.

"My men," Ballantine seethed "Are out there rescuing my daughter. If I sent a fucking battalion to do it, you would follow the damn orders and thank me for it."

The muscles in the General's jaw clenched, but he nodded again.

"I'm glad we cleared that up."

Ballantine walked back to the Comm monitors and watched.

"That's all," he said over his shoulder to the military man.

He didn't turn around as the General slunk from the room.

"Mr. Ballantine?"

"What is it!" he snarled at Del.

"We've lost them."

7

7

"Move! Move!"

"God damn Z everywhere!

He pulled the trigger on his rifle in short three round bursts.

"Single shot!" he screamed to his men.

They were limited on ammunition, so it wouldn't do to blow all their wad in one firefight.

Better to use auto to clear some space, then single shot to make a hole and escape through the line.

The formation was tight on him as they moved down the street.

The move bought them a little time, though the zombies were still stalking them, relentless. Terminal.

"Get me a lead on our direction," he shouted to his second.

Javi pulled a map in a plastic pouch from a pocket on his vest and coordinated their position with a street sign.

"This way, four klicks."

Sharp motioned him to point and the rest of the men fell in line one arm's length behind.

Still the Z kept coming.

They ambled out of the dark spaces between houses and filled the street, turning it into a gauntlet of grasping hands and gnashing teeth.

The soldiers ran the gauntlet, shooting to keep the hole open.

They couldn't last forever, they needed to get clear.

Sharp reached into his fanny pack and lifted a grenade.

It was a small baseball size sphere, but packed with an incendiary charge by the boys in science.

Z liked fire and the fireball made a big one.

Maybe it would draw some of them off.

He stopped short, popped the pin and lobbed the grenade through the window of the house.

Then he was running again, pulling the rest of the men along with him as they fought to get clear.

The grenade exploded in a gush of flame that blew out windows of the neighboring homes.

Flaming curtains floated through the air as debris settled in the yard, but the bomb did the trick.

Fire flickered through the shattered windows and licked against the dry wooden structure.

It climbed higher, dancing across the roof.

That did the trick.

It drew off the first zombie, then another.

More followed, and it was enough to make the path a little clearer.

It wasn't much.

The men were still moving and the Z were still in the way, but their attention was divided.

It was all the squad needed to bolt for safety.

"Through the yard," Sharp shouted.

Javi led them between two houses, across a backyard.

They were up and over a fence, putting a barrier between them and the trailing Z.

The squad disappeared around another corner and found the way clear.

"Got a bead on that jet?"

Georgie pointed.

"Three klicks."

"Let's move."

The men kept close formation as they ran up the street, rifles raised and eyes up for zombies.

8

8

She wasn't sure where they were taking her so she kept quiet and watched everything as she was led out of the two-story brick building and onto a street.

The street lights were out.

It surprised her, though she knew it shouldn't have.

Even in New York, they were on electrical restrictions.

An influx of refugees from the cities that bordered the wall, and people who were able to make it out of the interior put a huge strain on resources, including electric.

There was a push by the Council to work up solar grids on

rooftops, but that would mean moving the tent cities that had been erected on top of buildings.

So, there were no streetlights in NYC, or anywhere after.

But there was ambient light that leaked through windows, and created blocks of pale shadows on the street.

Here, they used torches.

They were bolted to old flag holders, long thin poles wrapped in rags and soaked in some slow burning fuel.

The torches weren't spaced evenly, just enough to shine on a path that led to a smaller building.

The black man from the hospital stood on the short steps waiting for her.

"Up and about."

His smile was charming if guarded.
  She nodded.

"Sorry about your friend."

Pam shook her head.

"I didn't know her. We were on the plane together."

"I wasn't sure if we would be able to rescue you when we saw you land," he explained and ushered her through the door.

"By the time we arrived you were the only one who hadn't been bitten."

"Thank you."

"Don't thank me yet. You're the first survivor we've seen in a long time. And the first one who ever came in on a plane. We have a lot of questions for you."

He led her into a room and she stopped to gape.

She hadn't seen the back of the building in the darkness, but the small front was just that.

A façade.

She stood at the edge of a large auditorium, filled with the quiet murmurs of a packed crowd.

There was a sea of faces staring at her, thousands of them, and as she stepped out onto a stage, the crowd went silent.

Pam felt like she had landed in a science fiction movie.

She was from the City. Nothing was ever this quiet.

She lifted a nervous hand and waved.

Someone started clapping. It was picked up by dozens, then

hundreds of others.

She let the applause wash over her and tried to look strong.

Part of it was because she wasn't sure what everyone was clapping about, or why they were clapping for her.

Maybe they were just glad she survived.

Anyone survived.

But a thought dawned on her and she let it light a smile on her face.

They were clapping because she was from outside.

She came in on a plane, and that gave them hope.

These people looked like they needed hope.

The black man moved up beside her and spoke over the sound of the crowd.

"I'm Jacob. I'm in charge here."

"Pam."

"Take it in Pam," he advised. "Because once they're done, we get to the questions."

He didn't wait for them to finish.

Jacob waved them to silence.

"Can everyone hear?"

Someone from the back shouted to indicate the acoustics were good.

"I was going to start this by saying as some of you know, but judging by the size of our group, I think you all know who this young woman is."

Random laughter punctuated the crowd.

"I haven't seen all of you here in quite some time, but before I turn it into a lecture on civic duty, let's get some information. Would that work for everyone?"

Pam admired the way he handled the crowd, the easygoing tone that assured them he had their best interest at heart.

He turned to her.

"What's your name?"

"Pam. Pam Ballantine."

"Hello Pam," some of the crowd said together.

She waved again.

That opened the floodgate.

"Where are you from?"

"We haven't seen a plane in months."

"Where is everyone?"

"Is it like this everywhere?"

They were all shouting, voices raised louder to be heard over each other and it was chaos.

She held up her hands and brushed a stray strand of curly hair away from her eyes.

"Hold on, hold on."

"Yeah, people damn," the tall black man moved onto the stage next to her. "She just survived an attack by the walking dead. Let the woman breath."

"Thank you."

"Oh, don't thank me yet. You still got a lot of questions to answer. I just bought you a little time, that's all."

Pam took a deep breath.

"I could use time."

She pointed to the woman closest to the bottom of the porch steps.

"Alright you, what was your question?"

"Are there more survivors?"

"Yes," Pam answered. "I came from New York and I was going to Los Angeles. They've been affected by the infection too, but they're still standing."

"How many?"

Pam shrugged.

"I don't know an official count. I don't think anyone does, yet. We don't know how many we lost inside the wall, or how many made it to one of the refugee centers before we closed it."

"What's going on?!" a man in the back screamed. "When are they going to save us?"

"I don't know," Pam sighed. "I don't think anyone is coming to save you."

That set off new murmurs in the crowd, people in the middle shoving. Pam could see a distinct line down the middle as people took up sides.

She couldn't blame them. This confusion was everywhere. It was the reason her father created the Council, the reason he ran it with an iron fist.

Pam glanced at Jacob. She admired the way he had spoken to the crowd earlier, but now he just stood back and let them argue.

He didn't have an iron fist.

Maybe no fist at all.

"People!" she shouted. "People!"

They stopped. Mostly.

"I don't have all the answers," she said. "There are big questions you have, big questions you want to know about. But I will tell you what I do know. We think it started in Florida."

The crowd listened as she told them about Florida, and the spread. How the government collapsed and a group took control to save humanity.

"What about the Army?"

"Gone," she said.

"All of them?"

"We still have the coasts, and some survived. Just like some plumbers survived, some carpenters, and some salesmen. But all of the military was on the front lines in the zombie war."

She let that sink in. Americans had a vision of their military as being unstoppable.

She just told them most of it was gone.

And that meant no one was going to come help them.

"We're on our own?" a woman said in a soft voice that carried across the room.

Pam glanced at Jacob, but he hung his head.

"We're on our own," Pam answered. But she kept her head held high.

9

9

"Does that look empty to you Captain? Cause from where I'm standing that looks like a metric fuckton of zombie."

Sharp glanced up at the man who stood head and shoulders of everyone else in the squad.

"If I was a betting man Bear."

"I'm betting they're ain't nobody left alive in there."

"How about out here?"

Sharp called to Specs, their sniper as the man cast about for a trail.

"Somebody was out here. More than a couple."

"How many more?"

The short man squinted up at him.

"Hard to say Sir. Z been through here and scuffed it all to hell. I can see boo coo footprints going," he stood and pointed with the tip of his rifle away from the plane.

"Thataway."

"You trying out for a Western?"

"Been watching a lot of John Ford back at the FOB."

"Good work."

"There's a shoe in with the boots. Kinda small."

"Like a woman small?"

SPECS shrugged.

"Maybe a woman small."

Sharp noted the Z making note of them and he rallied his men to move out.

"Let's go see where they lead."

10

10

10

"Tell me about this place," she said.

She and Jacob stood on the porch in front of the auditorium after the meeting let out.

There wasn't much more she could tell them, she thought.

Outside the wall, they were safer. Right now, they were surrounded, isolated and alone in a vast wilderness full of zombies.

At least on the outside, there were no more Z, unless someone died or was killed.

Even then the Council had organized responses, and her father had made sure the SOP's, standard operating procedures were in place, known and practiced.

The elderly were monitored in their homes, bars had emergency call buttons to summon a response team if someone was shot or stabbed in a fight.

Hospital staff were trained on Z prevention, which was a nice way of saying they taught nurses how to shove a long thin icepick through the eyeball of the recently deceased.

"What are you a reporter?"

He said it in jest but there was an edge to his voice that made her raise an eyebrow.

"Sorry," he apologized. "Things have been a little tense of late."

"Yeah, surviving a plane crash and zombie overrun is a relaxing way to spend a Sunday afternoon."

"Is it Sunday?"

"You guys don't have a calendar?"

"To be honest we don't keep up with it in here because it's not important. Sunrise, try to keep everyone fed and alive. Sunset, try to make it through the night. A zombie apocalypse can make you fairly myopic."

"I call that Darwin's rule. A fight to survive."

"I don't think Mr. Darwin envisioned zombies as an evolution-ary step."

He poured water from a pitcher into a glass and set it beside her on the end table. She took a tentative sip and grimaced.

"Rainwater," he shrugged. "We put barrels under the down-spouts to catch all we can. People are used to running water, but when there's no power to prime the pumps we make due."

"Tastes better than New York water," she took another sip.

The man nodded.

He knew she was lying, but it was a little white lie of intended kindness. He appreciated the gesture.

"I was a city councilman for our fair town, one of six. I know that may sound small to you compared to the Big Apple, but we were content with our little disputes. Arguing over a stop sign versus traffic light seems so trivial now."

"I think a lot would seem trivial now, at least inside the walls."

"What made them pick the lines? I suppose if we thought about it, the mountains are natural barriers but putting walls up on the mountains would seem a daunting task."

"My father thrives on the impossible," she said with a hint of pride.

"Was your father a man of the people?"

"No," she grinned. "He hated people. He hates people. He was the head of a company that owned a television network. But what he is good at is leading. Leadership."

"It is an art," Jacob sighed. "One I am learning through the University of hard knocks."

"They elected you?"

"I came to it by default. Most people in a time of crisis look to someone they can lay the blame on if things go wrong. I'm in the winning spot of the blame game."

"It can't be that bad."

"It is. And worse. There are two factions behind our gates. One makes it almost impossible to live with the other, yet both sides must work together to survive."

"It's like that even outside the walls," she said. "People are scared. They're confused and don't know what to do. Everyone has lost so much."
Jacob didn't answer then. His eyes grew sad and misty, and she thought he was thinking of all he had lost.

It had been worse for them in here, of course it had.

Worse than even she could imagine, because her father was still alive, her friends in the City were still alive, and it was easy to go on living almost as they had before the zombie plague.

10

Places were less crowded, and the restaurants didn't always serve what they had listed on old pre-Z menus.

There were far fewer people on the streets, because even the survivors who lived outside the walls felt safer hiding indoors.

The television only showed news and education programs, per her father and the Council, she knew.

But there were DVD's galore, and she had even turned back to reading, starting on the classics she had read in middle school and working forward.

It was a way to pass the time, listening to music, watching programs and waiting.

Only Pam wasn't sure what she was waiting for.

She wasn't sure the rest of the world knew either.

Were they waiting for another outbreak?

For a scream in the night that indicated a death squad needed to come in and remove a Z from someone who had died a natural death?

Or were they waiting for a cure?

"The CDC was lost," she said out loud and on accident.

She didn't mean to say it, but her thoughts had slipped the veil of conversation, that fine line where a person is thinking along one track and discussing another with someone else, the two cross streams.

"They were working on a cure?"

It sounded more like a statement than a question.

"I don't know."

"That's what one faction thinks. I don't like the names, but they're called Z-tards or Z-flakes by the others."

"Drawn on old party lines," she said.

Jacob nodded.

"How we like our tribes. It's human nature, but that's part of the problem. People think humans are benevolent or kind because they witness acts of kindness and think that's who everyone is. Or should be."

"You don't believe in kindness?"

"Let's just say I believe in pragmatic acts, and sometimes those can be construed as a kindness. Right now, in this place, my job is to convince everyone to believe in survival."

"What do you do to those who don't?"

"A lot of hippies survived. There was an off-grid commune not too far from here and we took them in because we needed their skills. A lot of survivalists lived up to their namesake. We took them in to help protect us. We needed their skills also. But this city is a house divided."

"This country is divided. Literally. Two walls and a great expanse of the middle."

"Do you have zombie agitators in the cities? People who protest that the Z are people and deserve rights?"

"We've had a lot of demonstrations," she chose her words carefully.

Those demonstrations had turned to riots, and every single time, someone was killed and turned Z.

Her father instructed the Governor of New York to declare martial law and did the same in Los Angeles. She assumed it was like that in every city.

People were scared.
  They were hungry.

They were heartbroken, because a lot of them lost a loved one, or loved ones when the outbreak happened.

It was easy to blame the Z-sympathizers, but no amount of flower power was going to bring back the dead, or save them.

"I try to keep it simple in here," Jacob explained. "No Z pets. No harboring family until they find a cure. All Zombies are persona non-gratis in the compound."

"You've had people try to break those rules?"
"They aren't rules. They're law. Written in stone like the ten commandments and thou shall not break them upon penalty of expulsion. I'm serious about keeping people safe. Even if it's from themselves."

"I think you'd like my father," she chuckled.
"I don't know why I said that. You'd hate him. Everyone hates him. But you would respect his position on keeping people safe."

"People often hate those in power, or who wield it. Speaking of," Jacob nodded to a shadow moving across the yard.

A short round woman stopped at the bottom of the stairs and fought to catch her breath.

"Jacob," she wheezed. "We've got a problem."

11

11

Jacob and Pam ran after the rotund woman as she led them toward the city gate.

A crowd gathered on the walkways that looked down at the road outside, and a smaller group ringed the twelve-foot metal doors.

Pam saw lots of black hoodies and tie-dyed shirts.

She also saw guns aimed at the crowd and holding them back.

Jacob pushed to the front of the group.

"Hey Mike," he said in his calm soothing voice.

"Jacob," the gray-haired man who seemed to be leading the hoodie and tie dyed group answered.

"What's going on?"

"Michael's out there. I'm going to get him."

Jacob sighed.
   "I can't let you do that Mike."

"He's my son."

"I know," Jacob hung his head. "But we're not letting any Zombies inside the gate."

"Laura's with him."

He was almost sobbing. Jacob reached out to put a hand on his shoulder, but Mike jerked out of the way.

"I'm bringing them inside."

Mike moved for the gate. Jacob reached out to grab him, but a long haired freaky person shoved a rifle into his chest and pushed him back.

One of the gate guards jacked a shell into his shotgun and aimed into the tie-dyed crowd.

More weapons were drawn, cocked and aimed, but no one shot.

"Don't!" Jacob yelled. "Wait!"

He tried to calm them down, tried to get the crowd to focus on him instead of shooting each other.

Mike took advantage of the distraction. He wormed through the shoulders and people, reached the gate and cracked it open.

He dashed through the narrow slot and whooped as he ran down the road toward the shuffling remains of his family.

His yell caught the attention of other Z and they all started moving toward him.

Mike picked up a discarded branch, almost as long as he was and used it to fend off the zombies.

He didn't hit them, just herded and pushed them back.

Jacob shoved between the crowd and reached the walkway.

"Get that gate closed!"

Several of the men bullied their way past the guns to hit the gates and shoulder them closed.

"They don't know what they're doing Jacob, they're sick," Mike called in a sob.

He used the pole to push the teenage boy back from him, a gentle shove that kept the zombie from biting his face.

"We can't kill them, and I won't let them stay out here to rot. I want them inside where I can care for them."

"Get back in here Mike," Jacob called down from the walk. "We can talk about it inside."

"No!" Mike shouted up at him. "We're done talking. All you riflethumpers want to do is talk. The time for talk is over. It's time for action."

"Your people have rifles, Mike."

"You forced our hand. You made us do this. And now we know the world is still out there, that people are still alive, we know they're working on a cure. They can save our families."

Jacob cast a sideways glance at Pam and motioned her up to join him.

"Tell them."

"What?"

"Tell them there is no cure."

Mike grunted as he pushed the zombie formerly known as his wife away and shoved back two others.

"The CDC didn't survive," Pam yelled.

"How do you know? Did you know we were here?"

He was right. She didn't know. Not for sure. And she wasn't sure if anyone knew, really.

"I don't," she told him. "This happened so fast and we were trying to keep people safe. Even while we fought the Z ourselves."

"They're our family," Mike screamed. "Why can't you see that? Just say it. You know they are people."

"Zombies are not people," she raged back.
  "They're dead."

"Open the gate!"

"No!" Jacob yelled.

The hippies at the gate grabbed Jacob's men and pulled them away. They cracked it open.

They used the tips of their stolen weapons to shove the crowd further back, buying space and room to pull the gates in and open the road to the zombie swarm.

Mike cheered as he saw the crack in the wall.

He cheered again at the sight of his comrades welcoming him through, waving their arms to invite him back inside.

The boy Z, the one that had been Mike's son slipped under the stick he was using to hold them back.

The Z grabbed him by the collar and yanked his father off balance. They both fell to the ground, one moaning, one screaming.

The Z swarmed the gates.

There were too many of them for the untrained crowd to handle.

The guards were too far back, held in check by hippie guns, and now those same guns were silent, shocked and frozen by speed and tenacity of the herd.

It was an overwhelming thing, a powerful relentless mass of arms, teeth and moaning maws.

Mike screamed for help, screamed for mercy as his son gnawed a hole in his neck.

The boy's head exploded.

Then another.

Bullets ripped out of the darkness and shattered the zombie assault.

Soldiers advanced in a two by two formation, rifles held to shoulders as they sent single shots into the brainpans of zombies.

Bodies splatted on the ground.

11

They approached from the side, rather than the back, a finely drilled point that cut a path through the swarming bodies, leaving a pile of twitching half rotten corpses in their wake.

The soldiers moved to the gate.

Sharp switched his aim inside and cleared the first row of Z from behind.

The second row spread out, and the sudden appearance of the fighting force moved the guards inside to action.

They knocked the hippie insurrection aside, ripped the weapons from their hands and began shooting zombies too, taking back the town.
   Georgie planted his back against a corner hinge on the gate, switched to full auto and lay down a line of fire that decimated the zombie front.

Doc joined him from the opposite gate and thirty seconds later, the road was clear for twenty yards.

The squad moved through and forced the gate closed from the inside.

Then it was a simple mop up exercise to eliminate the rest of the intruders.

"Georgie, Spec, up top and keep me
   apprised," Sharp ordered.

The two men scrambled up the walkway and set up watch on either side of the closed gate.

Sharp stepped over a twitching body and eyed the crowd.

"Good thing we got here when we did," he pulled a Kbar from a sheath and stabbed the dead hippie in the brain before it could turn Z.

There were a dozen civilian casualties.
    He noted the other armed men moving through the injured and deceased, dispatching them in a manner similar to the one he used.

"I'm looking for Pam Ballantine," Sharp called out. "Who's in charge of this clusterfuck?"

Jacob stepped forward and motioned with one hand.

"I'd object to your calling it a cluster because it only just happened, but whatever you name it, I'm in charge of it."

"Outstanding," said Sharp.

He eyed the woman who stood beside Jacob.

"I'm Pam Ballantine."

"Captain Sharp, Ma 'me. We're here to rescue you."

12

12

He wasn't used to them telling him no.

He wasn't used to anyone saying no except as a bargaining tactic.

No meant offer more money.

No meant use a different tactic.

No meant whisper a threat.

Then no would change to yes.

But the Council didn't budge.

The Chambers were eighteen floors below his office and he seethed every step back up.

His assistant could barely keep pace, and he noted that she at least wore flats instead of wobbly heels this time.

Good.

The woman learned.

He liked it when people learned from him without having to point it out.

His seething served a purpose.

Ballantine knew that anger held in check could be made useful, but he also knew that his personality type was prone to violent outbursts.

The exertion on the stairs curbed that aggression, and let him wallow in self-pity, rage and anger for the time it took to make it back to his office.

He grabbed a linen cloth off from the top drawer of the desk and wiped his sweaty brow.

"Water," he ordered.

His assistant hopped to comply.

Now that he was spent, he could still feel the anger percolate in his gut, but his mind was clear.

The Council didn't want to send another group of military men after his daughter.

They lost radio contact with her plane and now the rescue squad had them afraid.

They feared the worst.

But Ballantine refused to accept that his Pam was dead.

She couldn't be dead.

It was inconceivable.

She was his progeny, wily and smart.

Even if everyone else died in the crash, he had heard her voice on the radio.

She had kept her head enough to call for help.

Her next step would be go to ground and wait.

She knew her message would reach her father and that he would move the earth to send help to her.

So she would wait.

Since the military failed, and the Council wouldn't send more, he would have to seek alternative measures.

He fell into the leather seat as his assistant poured a glass of Evian across filtered ice cubes into a crystal glass and set it beside him.

He reached up without looking and moved it to a coaster on the desktop to prevent a moisture ring.

"I need a street person," he mused. "Do I know anyone from the mean streets of Los Angeles?"

He didn't look at her.

He didn't even really realize she was there, he was just thinking out loud.

"My brother," she squeaked.

Ballantine glanced up in surprise.
   "Who?"

"My brother is- or he knows," she stumbled.

He turned around and glared at her.

"What is it?" he barked.

She jumped.

"My brother knows certain people," she

squirmed. "he's in the black market."

The black market.

That's what he needed.

Ballantine knew it existed, and he allowed it at his leisure knowing there were things he could not control about human nature.

Ban a book, and that's all people wanted.

The black market was for things he could not provide, certain food stuffs, drugs, items that once came from the middle of America too, but were now in limited supply.

"What does your brother do for this black market?"

She shrugged. It was maddening.

"I don't know."

Ballantine sighed.

"Alright, tell me what you do know."

She started to speak and he cut her off.

"Better yet, get him up here."

"Sir?"

"You heard me. Get his ass up here now."

She nodded and flinched through the door.
  Ballantine sat behind his desk and sipped the water.

A plan had percolated up through the rage and now that he had a target and direction, he knew where to aim it for the most effective use.

13

13

The woman turned to a tall black man next to her and smirked.

"Told you my Dad would take care of it."

Jacob didn't seem so sure.

He stared at the soldiers with a mixture of shock and awe, as if they were ghosts.

"I'm Jacob Williams," he said. "I'm in charge of this cluster."

Bear pointed at the metal doors that were being wedged shut.

"Your gate design is wrong. They should push out, not open in. If you reverse the hinges, the weight of the Z pressing on the doors will keep them sealed shut. Right now, it's just a matter of leverage before they get through."

Jacob looked past him to the gates.

They were holding, for now.

But he could see a thin line between the two plates and even as he watched it slipped a fraction wider.

"Let's get some girders against it," he called to some of the people around him.

No one moved.

They stared at the soldiers, looks of relief on their faces.

The government was here, they were armed.

The wait was over. They were going to be saved.

Sharp could hear their murmurs, feel their stares.

He twirled his finger in the air and rounded his squad up on him.

"Stay close," he muttered out of the side of his mouth. "When they find out we're only here for her."

He let it stand.

The men knew how desperate a crowd could get, and if the mob mentality took over, it might call for killing civilians.

They wanted to avoid that if they could.

"Ma'am," Sharp nodded to Pam. "Let's get inside and talk."

"I'm afraid we can't go inside yet, Captain. Jacob has a problem and he needs to resolve it, or that group might try to open the gate again."

She turned to Jacob with an expectant look on her face.

He nodded and bowed his head.

"People," he said in a deep voice. "You saw what happened to Mike. You saw how these men responded. It was only with their help that we were saved. You can't continue this course of co-existence. The things out there will kill you, kill us. Do you want to be responsible for all of our deaths?"

"Mike was right!" screamed a woman. "My husband is still out there. He's sick."

"We just need to learn how to communicate with them," some-one else shouted.

"Dead lovers!" shouted a man behind Jacob.

Others took up his scream, and then nothing could be under-stood as each side tried to make their point with threats, noise and chaos.

Jacob raised his hands for quiet. They ignored him.

Even when Pam moved beside him, they ignored her.

A couple of the flower power group moved on the gate, intent on opening it again, or maybe just blocking it with their bodies and hosting a peaceful protest under the moans and groans that leaked through the opening.

Sharp raised his rifle and fired off two rounds.

A few people screamed. Others ducked.

Some of the smarter ones ran for their houses.

But the rest shut up and stared at him.

"Keep this area clear," he instructed Bear. "No one touches that gate."

The giant soldier nodded and planted himself in the middle of the road.

It might have been his immense size.

Or the weapon he held at the ready.

But everyone backed up and backed off.

13

Sharp turned to Pam.

"We're talking. Now. Bring him."

14

14

Ballantine looked up from his desk as his assistant led a handsome young man into his office.

He liked this moment almost more than any other.

The look on their face when they saw the vast amount of space that dwarfed his giant desk, all of it just for him.

Space was a premium, and in some areas, a currency, and here it all belonged to him.

That was a show of true power.

He was not disappointed.

14

The young man shuffle stepped, almost off balance, but he recovered and marched as if he never lost confidence.

There was no place to sit so he stood in front of Ballantine and waited.

"Mr. Ballantine," her soft voice broke the silence as the two men stared at each other across the expanse of his desk. "This is my brother, Mickey. I think he can help you get what you want."

She backed away, introductions complete.
 Mickey winked at her before she shut the door.

"I've heard a lot about you," he said.

"I imagine you have. Whereas I have heard nothing about you."

"That's just the way I like it."

Ballantine detected a low trace of the Irish in his voice. Mickey and his sister must be one, maybe two generations removed from immigrants he thought. She's younger, so more time in American schools would have erased most of her accent.

He spent a moment trying to recall if she held a lilt on certain words, then shook it off.

The tangent was unimportant.

What was important was the business of getting down to

business. He didn't bother with the niceties of offering a drink.

"I have a business proposition for you."

"I'm here aren't I?"

Cocky, Ballantine mused. Probably served him well with the types of people he dealt with on a day to day basis.

He had been accused of arrogance many times in the past, and he supposed those people were not wrong.

The difference was he had the power to back it up.

He wondered if this young man did as well.

"I'm told you are a man who can procure things."

"Why don't we dispense with the foreplay Mr. Ballantine."

"Excellent. You can get things."

"Things. Many of the things we have left."

"And people?"

"A little harder, but it can be done."

"I want you to get me an army of mercenaries to go fetch my daughter."

"Kidnapping? We ain't into kidnapping."

"This isn't a kidnapping," Ballantine explained. "It's a rescue."

"Where is she? Are you having a little trouble with the San Francisco Council."

"I don't have trouble with the Council."

The way he said it almost made the gangster shiver. He'd been in the presence of men like this before.

They were usually the boss and with good reason.

The last man that looked at him like that beat three other men in the room to death with a baseball bat during a lunch meeting.

It had been a scene in his favorite movie about Al Capone, until he saw it happen live.

Now he couldn't even watch baseball on television.

Or couldn't watch baseball on television until the Z attacked.

If he had the chance at anything other than DVD movies and public service announcements, he'd watch baseball for hours.

"Sir," he said to indicate his respect. "What service can I provide."

The blaze in Ballantine's eyes receded to a dull roar and the palpable tension in the room relaxed a notch.

Mickey felt like he had just avoided the jaws of a great predator and suppressed a shudder again.

"Your sister has led me to believe you are in the black market."

Normally he would mince words and try to dance around the truth, but if that look came back in the man's eyes, he wasn't sure if he would make it from the building alive.

So, Mickey did something he that would have surprised the men he worked with.
    He told the simple truth.

"I am the black market," he confessed. "Or a part of it."

"Which part."

"Drugs. Women. Weapons."

"Women?"

"There are plenty of men willing to trade for companionship, and a lot of women who don't enjoy going hungry, Sir."

"The Council provides food," Ballantine argued.

"Yes," Mickey nodded. "They give out some food. Sometimes it even makes it to the right hands."

The blaze flickered up again.

Mickey wondered what he had said wrong and glanced at the window.

"Someone is stealing from me?"

The gangster gulped. He wasn't going to turn on his compatriots, because if word got out that he had, a twenty second trip to the concrete below would be a welcome relief compared to what would be done to him.

He kept his face passive, neutral.

Ballantine wrestled for control and took a deep breath.

"We will discuss that for another time."

Mickey watched his white knuckles pop out as he gripped the edge of the desk.

"You said weapons. Do you have men who can use them?"

Mickey nodded.

"I want a group of them to go get my daughter."

Mickey nodded again.

"Time and place. I'll do this service for you."

"Of course, you will," Ballantine grimaced a smile. "It's cute you thought you had a choice."

"When. Where."

It was all he could trust his voice to say without showing too much fear.

"Kansas. I'll draw you a map."

Then he did show fear.

"That's over the wall," Mickey stammered.

"That's right."

"No one goes beyond anymore. It's not done. How did she get in Kansas?"
   Ballantine eased back in his seat.

"She was flying from New York and the plane landed. Not a crash, but a landing. She radioed me for help."

"The military," Mickey licked his lips.

"Tried. Failed. They jumped in on parachutes and we lost their signal."

Mickey glanced at the window again.

He wondered if it would hurt when the glass shattered, or if the pane was stronger up here.

Would he bounce back and then have to be tossed again?

"If they can't help her," he stuttered.
  "She's not dead!"

Ballantine's fist slammed against the desk.

Mickey almost fell over backwards.

"Mr. Ballantine," he said. "This is too much."
  "No. It's just enough. You said you have weapons. Get more. You said you have men. Get more. I can't get you a plane, so you need transportation. I'll get you through the wall, you go get her and bring her back."

"Drive?"

"Unless you have another idea?"

Christ almighty the man was mad.

He wanted Mickey to take a group of men across the country in a truck through a zombie filled wasteland to save one girl.

"It can't be done."

"Mr. O'Rourke," Ballantine leaned up again.

His piercing blue eyes locked Mickey to his seat.

"I don't believe in the impossible. I saved half this god damn country from zombies, and now I'm asking for a little payback. If I say you can drive across the fucking desert and pick her up, you're going to go get every god damn person out there and take them with you to do it."

They stared at each other, but it was no contest of will, no battle of spirt.

Mickey knew he wouldn't win that way.

But he was a good negotiator.

He had learned from the best in Chinatown working his way around the fringes of gang controlled territory there.

The Chinese never accepted the first offer, and never made an offer that had to be accepted.

He had found that to be true in all the men he dealt with.

It was only in the movies where they made offers that couldn't be refused.

This man wanted something from him.

He wanted something in return.

"I'll do what you ask," he said with a little more confidence. "But when I do, I'll be wanting something in return."

"Terms," Ballantine grinned.

Mickey was reminded of a shark's large white teeth and what they would do to a man.

He swallowed hard.

"I want a seat on the Council."

"Done."

That simple.

The man didn't need to consult, didn't dicker.

He just clapped his hands together and the decision was made.

"You return with my daughter safe and whole, and you'll have a seat on the Council."

He stood and held out a hand.

"Gather your best men. As many as you need. Get the resources together and let your sister know how you plan to cross. I want you out of here and on your way today."

Mickey looked at the window.

It would be dark in four more hours.

"I can get us ready to go today, but kitting up will take time. I need twelve hours."

Ballantine squinted and snarled.

"I don't like the delay."

"It's not a no, Mr. Ballantine. It's an issue of logistics. I have to find men I can trust, who have experience and get the supplies kitted up. We have to commandeer vehicles, pack them with food to last."

"Fine."

"I'd leave right now if you had it ready," Mickey offered. "Do you have a truck ready to go."

Ballantine's hand fell.

"No."

"Don't you worry then. I'll see to it and I'll get your daughter back to you safe, Sir."
   Mickey stood and backed away.

"Mr. O'Rourke," Ballantine stopped him.

The gangster turned and flinched as the Councilman stalked across the room toward him.

He had almost escaped, he thought, and now it was a quick swan dive down.

But Ballantine took his hand and shook it.

"We're men who understand each other, aren't we? A hand-shake is a contract between the two of us."

He pumped his arm up and down twice and let go.

Mickey massaged his fingers and felt like he had just been in the jaws of a shark and escaped.

"We understand each other Sir."

Then he was free.

Mickey shot a look to his sister as he passed by, and gave her a reassuring wink.

She shrugged and mouthed the word
  "Sorry" before he hit the stairwell.

He couldn't blame her for bringing him in on this though.

It wasn't her fault that the man was impossible to refuse.

And now he had a big job ahead of him.

But the reward, the reward was worth it.

A seat on the Council.

15

15

Sharp allowed Jacob to lead them away from the crowd.

His men fell in after him, weapons still held ready.

The crowd didn't surge, but neither did they move.

The shock of soldiers surprised them, as did the loss of members of their community.

There was grumbling, the zombie sympathizers still concerned with the welfare of their undead family, but the specter of the well-armed squad dissuaded them from acting on it.

They moved back onto the porch where Jacob and Pam had first been summoned to the gate.

"Keep it private," Sharp ordered.

Georgie, Javi, and the squad deployed in a semi-circle around the yard to keep back anyone who might approach.

"We're glad you're okay Ma'am," Sharp started. "We'll get you out of here but our Com guy bought it on the landing."

He turned to Jacob.

"I need your radio."

The tall man shook his head.

"If we had a radio, don't you think we would have used it to call for help? Or listened in to know others were out there?"

Pam held up a hand to placate him.

"We didn't know you were here," she said, then frowned as she ducked her head. "We should have known. It only makes sense that there would be survivors, right?"

She turned to Sharp.

"There are probably hundreds of places like this stuck out here," she said. "People just trying to survive."

"Not my problem."

"Excuse me?" she blanched.

"I've got one problem. I don't have a way to contact your father to let him know you're alive. We're alive. We were supposed to ping in when we landed. They're going to assume the worst."

"There are US citizens out here," she snorted. "You're supposed to protect them."

"All due respect Ms. Ballantine, my mission is you. Anything else is outside my scope."

He turned to Jacob.

"I'm going to have my men take a look around, see if there's something we can use."

He opened the door, motioned for Javi.

"Send the men out by two's and find a radio tower or communications array we can use."

His Sergeant snapped a salute and turned to give the orders.

"I want to talk to you about your mission," Pam said from behind him.

Sharp stood and waited.

"You see how bad it is in here?"

He nodded.

"These people need our help. My father would help them."

Sharp shrugged his shoulders.

"What? You don't think he would?"

"I don't know your Dad," he said. "Not personally. But his reputation never stood out as someone who was looking out for everyone else."

"He saved you," she almost stamped her foot. "He saved the whole world."

Sharp nodded over her shoulder toward Jacob.

"Not the whole world."

Javi knocked on a post and peeked up.

"Cap, we got something."

16

16

That something was a cell tower a few miles away.

Two of his soldiers had climbed on the roof of a building and spied it in the distance.

Sharp jumped off the roof onto the top of a box trailer backed next to it, then down the cab of the truck to the ground.

He motioned the men over.

"That was some good thinking to get high," he praised them.

"Nothing Sir," said Jenkins, the younger of the two. "We used to climb tress at home just to see how far we could see."

"I wouldn't have thought of it, so way to keep your head."

He circled the rest of the squad around.

"This place doesn't have a communications center, so we're going to that tower and making a call home. They should send a plane to get us."

The men shifted, but didn't say anything.

Their mission was to retrieve Ballantine and return to the LZ.

Once the call went out, they would have a few hours until the plane landed, and then they would be back on their way behind the wall.

"What about these folks?" Bear asked.

"Not our mission."

Javi sniffed.

"That's a lot of people to leave out here."

"Which ones are you going to choose to go with us?" Sharp snapped.

"Maybe we could leave the ones who wanted to open the gates out here and just take the rest."

"Not our call. Not our job. What is our job?"

Sharp glared at the men.

He didn't like the idea of leaving a group of civilians behind any more than they did, but that wasn't his decision to make.

The decision had been made fifteen hundred miles away, and their poor pre-op planning didn't allow for this.

They should have known, should have anticipated what they would do if they ran into other survivors.

He was pissed at himself most of all.

There was no excuse.

He had no excuse.

The if/then scenario should have occurred to him.

Now things were moving fast.

He'd have time to sit down and think about it later, when he compiled the mission de-brief.

He'd let HQ know about the survivors in the community and the potential other communities scattered around the interior.

They could come up with a solution to find and rescue more people.

He wasn't sure where they would put them though.

LA was packed tight all the way up to the Sierras.

People living with people, people camped out in front yards, in back yards. Space was tight.

He was glad it wasn't his call to make.

Going to the cell tower was.

"We move in twenty minutes. I want that call to go out and get them here while we still have daylight. Everything goes right, we eat in the mess hall tonight."

That seemed to placate the men, if not satisfy them.

At least the scowls disappeared.

"Get to it," he sent them on their way.

"Captain?" Jacob waited at the corner of the building. "I think I might have something to help."

17

17

Jacob led a group of three rag clad civilians over to the waiting squad.

There were two men and a young woman, barely more than a girl.

They all looked tired, malnourished, and resentful.

"Got your people ready?"

"I just want to remind you Captain, they're not soldiers. They're civilians."

"You don't have to remind me of my job. Can they keep up? That's the only thing you can be concerned with."

"We can keep up," the older man said.

"Don't you worry about us," the young man added.

The girl said nothing. She chewed on a
  plastic straw, moving it from one corner of her mouth to the
next.

Sharp tried to suppress a sigh.

Attitudes, he thought.

"Tell me their specialties."

"I'm a telecom exec," the young man said.

"Computers," added the older man. "Chip. My name is Chip."

"Chip," Sharp motioned him to join Specs. "This is your battle
buddy. You don't move away from him. Copy me?"

"I'll watch the woman," Bear volunteered.

She switched the straw in her mouth again and snorted.

"You got a name sweetheart?" the giant rumbled.

"Yes," she said. "And it ain't sweetheart."

"I think she likes you Bear," Javi teased. "You. Einstein. Pop
over here and stick to my hip."

The young man moved to walk beside him as Sharp rallied the tiny group toward the gate.

"I'm Rodney."

"Sure you are Einstein. You're the brains behind this outfit, anyone can see that."

"Actually, I just know where the tower is located."

"We know where it is Einstein."

"I meant I'm from this town. I know the fastest way."

Javi punched him on the shoulder.

"Brains, map. Same difference to us. You get us there and don't get dead."

Sharp held them up at the gate.

"Once we're over that wall, there is a no talking rule. No talking, no shouting, no screaming. The only sound I want to hear is your bootsteps right behind mine. Questions?"

Einstein raised his hand.

"How am I going to direct you?"

Javi shook his head and dragged him to the front of the group.

"We're point, Einstein. We lead the way."

Bear drifted to the back of the squad, and kept the girl in front of him.

That left Sharp and Combine to play roamers and watch their flanks.

"We move low," he set the orders. "We move fast. If we encounter a group of Z, we avoid them. No heroics out there, got it?"

The other five soldiers gave him a yes sir.

Sharp motioned to Jenkins at the gate.

Jacob stood off to one side next to Pam and the rest of his men.

"Good luck," he called to them.

The gate opened to an empty road and Javi led the squad out into the open.

18

18

They should have rested overnight and set the mission for the morning, Sharp thought as he eyed his men.

They looked tired as they ran through the streets, civilians at their side.

The speed was called the Ranger shuffle, so named because they could keep going at that rate for hours and eat up the miles.

It was slow enough the civilians could keep up, but would get them across the city to the cell tower and back before twilight.

Or so he thought.

But he wanted his squad looking sharp in case of a fight, and by the sound of the Z's around them, it was something they couldn't avoid.

"Eyes sideways," Javi shouted.

Their heads swiveled to the road on the right following his indicated direction.

A small herd of Z shambled up the road, grouped together.

Sharp didn't have time to count them.

"Left flank," Bear called out.

He aimed his rifle to the left at another herd of Z.

More than twenty, less than fifty was all he had time to think.

They couldn't go back.

There were Z back there too, grouping not tight yet, but a gauntlet he didn't want to put them through, not with the civilians.

Besides, the way to the tower was still clear.

But when the three herds merged behind them, going back to the walled compound was going to be rough.

"Double time!"

The squad shifted into overdrive and hustled up the street.

The civilians kept pace. Being a zombie snack was a huge motivator to move.

Combine led them around the corner of the next street and it was a straight shot to the fenced enclosure around the base of the cell tower.

A dozen Z blocked the way.

"Cut them down?" Javi called.

Sharp gave them a negative. The bullets would draw more Z.

He slung his rifle and yanked out the long KBAR knife. Combine did the same while the others watched their charges.

Sharp would have preferred more distance between him and a walking dead man, but the nine-inch blade would have to do for quiet work.

He and Combine moved up the street whacking and stabbing the zombies and plopping their dead bodies off to the side.

They made short work of it just as the merged Z herd rounded the corner, a collective moan washing up the street.

"Move."

Sharp hustled them toward the tower enclosure.

"They're going to block us in Cap," Javi called as he glanced over his shoulder.

Sharp pulled up as they reached the fence gate.

"Bear," he directed.

The big man moved to the padlock on the latch. He reached into a pouch on his vest, removed a small butane torch and clicked it lit with a lighter.

The tiny blue flame cut through the padlock shaft and the metal body fell to the concrete with a muted clang.

"In," Bear stepped back.

"Combine, on me," said Sharp.

"Not a good idea Cap," Javi argued. "You baby sit the civvies, let me and Bear play hide and seek."

Sharp shook his head.

"No time to argue, Sgt. Get in there, shut the gate and we'll draw them off."

Combine squared off on his shoulder.

"Point the way, Captain."

Javi and Bear led the three civilians into the enclosure and slammed the gate home.

"We won't get all of them," Sharp said to him. "Keep them safe. Get the call out and get us a ride home."

"You get back to catch that ride."

Sharp grinned, slapped Combine on the shoulder and the two of them jogged away from the tower to where the road turned again.

They waved to get the Z's attention, and fired off two shots into the leading zombies just to be sure.

The herd shifted in their direction and began to follow the two men as they ran down the street.

Javi watched them go with a glare on his face.

"Get it done," he motioned to Chip.

The old man went to the base of the tower and tried the black box that was bolted to one of the legs.

"Locked," he shouted.

The noise drew a few Z toward the fence.

"Damn it," Javi said and moved away from the gate.

If they could hide behind the legs of the tower, he would make them. But there was nowhere that the Z couldn't see, or smell or whatever it was that they did.

Bear moved Chip to one side and sliced the lock off the box.

Chip opened the door and began to work on the components inside, crossing the wires and searching for a signal.

The crowd of Z around the fenced enclosure grew from a couple to a couple of dozen as more were drawn by the groaning moans of the others.

Javi was worried. He hadn't heard any more shots since the Captain and Combine ran off.

"How we living?" he called to Bear.

Bear studied the configuration Chip was trying to work on inside of the shelf.

"Almost got it," he said.

Bear looked over his shoulder. The inside was a collection of wires that led to a simple tiny screen that looked like a tablet hopped up on steroids.

Right now, a diagnostic was running on the components, and a tiny window with a keypad was open in the lower corner.

"He's almost got it," Bear repeated.

Javi gave the big man a tight grin.

"I heard him Bear."

"Wasn't sure," he shrugged. "These Z are pretty loud."

"Why don't you kill them?" Einstein's voice cracked as he said it.

"They can't kill them Rodney," said the girl.

Javi watched her move next to Chip.

"Almost got it Jess," the older man assured her.

She patted him on the shoulder and watched him work.

"Got it," he announced and stood back from the box.

Javi glanced inside and looked at the old man.

"How does it work?"

"I had to bounce the signal across a couple of old networks that were still up. We send out the message, and wait for them to respond."

"I don't need to know the guts, just what to do."

Chip nodded.

"Okay," he pointed. "You just type on the keyboard."

Javi let go of his rifle and moved his fingers across the keypad to type out a message.

"How do you send?"

"Press send," said Bear.

"If I saw a send key, I'd press it," Javi snapped.

"It's right there, Sarge."

Javi looked. The send key was right there on the bottom of the keypad. He shook his head and pressed the tip of his finger against it.

Nothing happened.

"Did it work?"

Chip gently pushed him aside and studied the screen.

"It's sent."

"I didn't hear a beep."

"It doesn't beep."

"It seems like it should beep," said the soldier.

Chip shrugged.

"I didn't make it."

"You would have added a beep though, right? So, people would know that it worked."

"Probably."

"Alright. What's next?"

"We wait for an answer."

"How long?"

"I don't know. How long will it take for them to make a decision?"

Javi didn't know, and Sharp wasn't around to ask.

Whoever got the message would have to go up the chain and that might take some time.

He moved to the front of the enclosure and stared past the growling zombies that blocked most of the view. He wished Sharp was here so they could talk it out.

19

19

She watched them come and go, the people of this town, passing her by with a wave and a smile.

There were more of them than she had suspected.

The ones at the town hall meeting, if that's what it could be, called were less than half if the numbers she counted in her head as they passed were true.

Every now and then she would see a familiar face, a hint of recognition that was rewarded with a smile or a nod. They must have seen her in the auditorium, and her subconscious mind must have made note of them.

It was like tiny flashes of déjà vu registering across her mind, lightning in a summer storm.

She wondered how they came to be here and knew there were a thousand stories that led to this moment, a thousand tragedies that forced them all together behind the steel walls.

She saw it time and again in NYC, and heard about it from her father.

He built the walls, he created the safe zones, and then once the doors were shut no one else was let in.

It was safer that way, no chance of bringing in someone hiding the Z plague.

She wondered if it was like that here at some point. Did they turn people away?

And she wondered how many other places like this were out here, trapped in the wastelands, struggling to survive.

"I would offer a penny for your thoughts," the white-haired man she had first seen in the hospital wing moved across the brown grass and sat next to her.

"But I'm afraid hard currency no longer has any value here."

She gave him a light smile.

"Your money is no good here."

"Literally," he studied her for a moment and she held his gaze.

"What's your name?"

"I didn't introduce myself in the hospital wing?"

"One of my co-passengers was trying to eat my face at the time."

"Silas."

"Hi Silas, I'm Pam."

She held out her hand and he took it in his long fingers with a strong firm grip. His skin was soft, no calluses.

"My thoughts were about this place," she told him. "How you got here, what's the story."

She said it like she didn't expect an answer, and if she did, he wasn't going to give her one.

"I don't dwell on history. I prefer to focus on the present, with an eye to the future."

She indicated the street with the tip of her chin.

"What do you see in the future here?"

He sighed and clasped his hands in front of him like he was about to pray and watched as a couple strolled by shoulder to shoulder.

"When you leave, we die."

That surprised her.

"How?"

"Not immediately. But the soldiers are here to get you. Just you. A rescue mission, if I'm correct. Not a refugee collection mission. And once you're gone, we starve. Or we die out, a few at a time. Either way, it's the future."

She wanted to argue with him, but he was right. The soldiers were here just for her. No one else was going back from this rescue.

She thought she could convince her father to mount a refugee mission to retrieve the members of this community.

But it would take time, and he might argue against it. If he took a stand against the effort, she might as well talk to the wall he built.

How many would die while they waited?

"Can you change that future," she asked.

Silas looked up from his hands.

"I think we're trying."

"Then you can prevent it."

"No, we can just delay it."

There was a sadness in his voice, but she couldn't narrow it down any further to specifics.

She felt like he was holding something back, holding on to something that he was afraid to share.

Before she could ask him more, he stood up and dusted off the bottom of his pants.

"We could make a plan," she said, but he held up a hand to stop her.

"Plans don't always work out the way you want them to," he held out his hand to shake hers again.

"It was nice to meet you Pam. We'll miss you when you're gone."

She watched him walk away and almost called out to stop him, to ask him more questions, but she didn't.

She bit her lip and thought. He was wrong about plans. She just needed the right one.

20

20

Combine and Sharp ran around the corner back toward the fenced in enclosure.

Even from the distance, Javi could see Combine laughing.

They pulled out their knives and came up behind the Z at the fence, working through them in a quick, efficient fashion.

Bear and Javi pulled their knives and joined them, and the squad made fast work of the remaining Z.

"What's so funny?"

"You should have seen Cap," said Combine. He wiped the gore

off his blade onto the crusty shirt of one of the fallen zombies, not that it did much good.

"We needed the herd to keep on moving, but we couldn't figure out how. Then he saw a riding lawn mower in a garage. He just started it up, killed a Z for its belt, and tied the steering wheel so it would go in a straight line. Sent it off down the road like a motorized pied piper pulling the zombies right along with it."

Javi nodded his head in appreciation.

"Good thinking, Cap."

Sharp glanced inside the black box.

"Sit rep?"

"We sent the message, now we're waiting for the answer."

"It's not in real time?"

"Can't," said Chip. "Not anymore. We don't have satellites to bounce the signal off of, or if we do, it would take too much time for me to find it and adjust the configuration. I moderated this into a radio signal, so it's going to reach them bouncing off other towers and receivers."

"Will it work?"

The older man shrugged.

"If they're listening."

Sharp knew they were listening. Even though he hadn't seen the communications center first hand, there were rumors enough about it.

Monitored 24/7/365 to stay in contact with the East Coast and other survivors.

"What are we doing Cap?"

"Waiting," he answered. "How will we know when they respond?"

"It doesn't ping," Javi explained.

"No ping?"

"No ding, no ping, no bell," said Chip.

"What about a whistle?"

"None of that either."

"How can you guys joke at a time like this?" Einstein shouted.

"Keep quiet," Sharp ordered. "You'll bring them back around."

Einstein hunkered down against the fence and pouted.

"We're stuck out here waiting to hear from who knows what

and you guys are making jokes."

"Relax man," said Bear. "Javi, get your guy."

"He's not my guy. You," he pointed at Jess. "Take care of him."

Jess sighed and pulled a machete from the belt at her waist. She stood up and lunged at Einstein.

He made a sound that was a cross between a cry and a whine as he ducked down, but she stopped before she got too close.

"You said take care of him," she joked with them.

Sharp let them have a quiet laugh, and then felt bad it was at the expense of the other man.

"Bear, Combine," he pointed them to police the perimeter. "Eyes out."

Then they waited.

21

21

Del stared at the board of lights and waited.

He'd done it. He'd asked her out for coffee and she said yes.

Now he just needed his shift to end and they could go. He was practicing being charming in his head when a hand fell on his shoulder.

He almost didn't jump.

"Startled you?" the General stood behind him and smiled.

Del gave a grin in return.

"I was concentrating on the board," he said. "Lost in my own little world."

The General studied the display with calculating eyes.

He knew the basics of how it worked, what they monitored, but this wasn't his domain.

Normally.

One of the red lights blinked green.

"What's that?"

He drew Del's attention to the monitor.

The Tech's fingers worked the keyboard and pulled up the signal.

"Radio contact," he said. "It's the extraction team."

"They're alive?"

"Yes Sir," said Del.

He reviewed protocol in his head, trying to decide who to contact next.

The first would be the Chairman, of course.

He would want to know the soldiers sent after his daughter were still alive and on mission.

The next message would be to Army command, but the head of that department was standing right behind him.

"Sir," Del explained. "SOP is send a message to you and the Chairman to inform you of the contact."

"We can deviate from that," the General patted him on the shoulder. "I'll save you a message."

"What about the Chairman?"

The General put his hand on his chin and stroked the lines next to his mouth.

"Set an extraction for the backup LZ," he instructed the Tech. "I'll inform the Chairman myself."

Del keyed the response in and sent the signal.

He didn't need to wait for an affirmation, those codes should have been keyed in the military's pre-communication briefing.

He glanced over his shoulder to the woman who watched him from several seats down, and gave her a victory smile.

The General was smiling too.

He planned to scramble the transport to pick up the Chairman's daughter and his team, then share the information with Ballantine so he could get the credit and accolades for it.

The man had embarrassed him before, but he now he had the chance to earn some favor back.

And in this new world, favors meant everything.

He slapped Del on the back again.

"Keep up the good work."

Del watched the General take his leave and caught her smiling at him again.

Did her grin hold just a little more promise than before she saw the highest-ranking member of the surviving military congratulate him?

He hoped so.

Del stared at the red lights on the communications array and thought a million thoughts about how the night might go.

22

22

"It's getting dark," Javi glanced at the sky. "How long do we wait?

"There's something coming in," Chip went to the box and scanned the tiny screen that showed the message.

"Backup LZ. 2200."

"They got it," crowed Bear.

"What's LZ?" Einstein pushed himself off the fence.

"Landing Zone at 11:00," Javi explained. "We're meeting them for a pick up."

"Good news?" Jess asked.

"Good news," Sharp confirmed.

He glanced at the sky and studied the descending twilight. They could make it back before it was full dark, and still reach the LZ in time.

"We gonna make it?" Javi checked in.

Sharp nodded and made a circling motion with his finger.

"We're going to move back fast and tight for the compound. Stay on your escort," he instructed the civilians.

"Keep them locked in and moving."

Combine opened the gate and led the squad through while Sharp brought up the rear and closed it behind them.

He was sure they would never come back once they made the plane, but it might come in handy for someone else, or in case Jacob needed to use it.

They ran in a tight group back toward the compound.

Combine rounded a corner and smashed headfirst into a row of Zombies crowded across the darkening street.

He didn't panic, and didn't scream, but squeezed off three rounds into the heads of two Z that were crawling up his legs.

The shots turned the rest of the Z.

Javi raced to Combine and hauled him to his feet, shooting short bursts into the lumbering dead.

Sharp grabbed Einstein and herded the rest of the civilians away from the threat, searching for another route.

"Get us back!"

Einstein was hyperventilating and the Captain screaming in his face didn't help.

"You said you were the map, get us back! Now!"

A zombie lurched out of the growing darkness grasping for their shoulders. Sharp twisted around and sent a bullet through its gaping mouth.

Einstein screamed. His eyes flitted around like a trapped animal and he bolted.

Sharp made a grab for him and missed.

"Bear!"

Bear lunged after him, the big man moving fast on his feet.

But he wasn't scared out of his wits, his brain dumping adrenaline into his system.

Einstein sprinted up the street back toward the enclosure, anywhere that was away from where the zombies were.

But it was too late.

They were surrounded.

He saw the shadowy forms in the growing darkness and tried to stop, but his feet slid out from under him.

Einstein bowled over two zombies who bit into his arm and shoulder.

Sharp raised his rifle to try and get off a shot, at least to put the man out of misery, but a Z head moved in the way and blocked his sight.

"Damn it!" he screamed.

His squad rallied around him.

"This way!" Chip screamed and pointed.

At least he was smart enough to stay in the middle of the armed men.

Maybe smart wasn't the right word, Sharp thought as he used single shot to clear a path.

Just more in control.

They moved in a tight formation up the street, each soldier

covering a quadrant and shooting a path through the zombies.

The group reached the road to the gate and it was clear.

The soldiers pulled a line behind the civilians and sent them running for the gate.

The squad backed up in step, keeping steady and controlled fire bursts to beat back the growing wave of growling Z.

They made it through the gates and watched in exhausted relief as it closed behind them.

"Get four men on the wall," Sharp ordered Javi. "Find us a distraction to draw them off so we have a clear path to the plane."

"Yes sir," Javi snapped and grabbed two of the newbies they had left behind to defend the compound.

"Bear, with me," Sharp grunted and went to find Pam as the big man fell in step behind him.

23

23

He found her with Jacob on the porch in front of the auditorium.

"Did you get through?" she asked.

"We lost one of your people," Sharp informed Jacob.

The town leader bowed his head and sent up a silent prayer.

"Which one?"

"The smart one," said Bear.

"Rodney."

"Damn," Jacob sighed. "I hope it was worth it."

"They're coming."

Pam clapped her hands together and rubbed them.

"I'm sorry for your loss," she said to Jacob. "But this is our chance to get the rest of your people to safety."

"There's room for all of us on the plane?"

"No," said Sharp. "There's not. There's room for the mission personnel."

"We can save all of these people."

"Not my job lady."

"Your job is to protect them."

"My job is to protect you and get you back to your father safe. That's it. Not one thing more."

"Then your job sucks."

"That may be true, and I think that sometimes, but right now, it's the only work I've got."

"I'm not going."

"Don't make me carry you."

"I'd like to see you try."

Sharp groaned. He didn't want it to come to this.

"Bear."

The giant moved in fast and scooped her up over his shoulder.

She barely had time to squeal before a massive forearm clamped down across her legs and pinned her to him.

She beat against his broad back, but it was like hitting a side of beef covered in Kevlar.

"You're only going to make yourself uncomfortable."

"Stop fighting," Sharp told her. "We're moving out."

"Now?" she stopped hitting Bear and tried to peer around at Sharp.

"Now. The plane is on the way."

"At least let me tell them good bye, and let them know I'm coming back to get them."

"No."

"No?"

"Too much blood rushing in your ears? I thought I was making myself clear."

"You can't tell me no, I don't take orders from you."

"Walk her out Bear."

The giant turned around and trundled toward the gate. Javi jogged behind him.

Jacob stood on the porch and watched them pass.

"This is for the best," he called out.

Sharp couldn't tell if it was a question or a statement.

24

24

Sharp and Bear made it to the gate again with a grumbling and squirming charge in tow.

"Did you get my distraction?" Sharp asked.

Javi nodded and pointed with his chin.

"Moved the main body of them to that side of the fence. We're going to have stragglers get in the way."

Sharp pulled the entire squad in close so they could hear him.

"We're making a run for the plane," he said. "The backup LZ may be hot, and we're going to have to make a path. Don't shoot unless you have no choice. Shooting draws them to us.

We move fast, we move quiet."

"Put. Me. Down," Pam squealed.

"We stay silent once the gate is open," Sharp said for her benefit.

"Once we're on the plane, we'll make a call for an airlift to get the rest of these people out of here. Coordinated and not on the fly."

That made Pam quiet down, or it could have been the blood rushing to her head.

"Put her down?" Bear asked.

"Not yet. We clear?" he called up to one of the compound guards that had replaced his men at the lookout by the gate.

The man gave him a thumbs up.

"We're green. Sgt., let's move out."

Javi turned the squad around and they moved out as the gates swung open.

The main mass of zombies had moved away, but there were stragglers still in their path.

The men jogged with quick precision, and quietly dispatched the moaning Z as they encountered them.

They kept the pace up until they reached the edge of town and then moved faster.

Bear set Pam down, helped her stay steady and then shadowed her as they ran with the others.

The backup landing zone was ten miles out of town on a long stretch of straight highway.

The trip to the LZ would have been gorgeous under different circumstances. Brilliant spots of sparkling starlight cascaded across the nighttime sky.

Since the zombie apocalypse, most of the electrical pollution that hid the expanse of the galaxies had disappeared.

No wonder all of the ancient cultures had advanced concepts of astronomy, Sharp thought as he listened to their boots on the asphalt.

The stars were wondrous, and with nothing to interfere, mesmerizing to watch and study.

He could imagine the ancients laying in flat fields, gazing up at the heavens and learning, noting the changes, the shifts in color and location.

It distracted him until he saw one of the stars moving.

"Is that our ride?" Georgie saw it too.

"Looks like they're ahead of schedule," Javi answered. "Not by much."

The plane banked to the south of them as the pilots searched for the roadway.

They had the coordinates plotted, but Sharp realized he and his men failed to consult the map.

"It's coming in," he said as he noticed they were in the middle of the longest, flattest stretch of the road.

They watched the pilot bank the giant C–130 and bank again as he lined up on the road they were on.

"Do you hear that?"

Sharp strained to listen, but it didn't sound like the whine of plane engines.

It sounded like a thumping motor with a low moaning growl underneath it.

"Captain?" Javi pointed.

He couldn't make out details at this distance.

But he could see a mass of shadows moving up the road toward them.

Led by a riding lawn mower.

24

"Son of a-"

"What the hell is that?"

"That is a lot of flocking zombies."

"That's what we're going to call them? A flock?"

"A herd? A stampeded? Whatever the fuck you want to call them, there are a lot of them."

"A metric fuckton?"

"A metric double fuckload."

"Incoming," Combine pointed.

The pilot had lined up on the road and was coming in on top of them.

The squad moved out of the way as the plane hit the highway and screeched past them.

It crushed the lawn mower and plowed into the herd of zombies.

Sharp watched the bodies clog the wheels around the jet, cover the road with a swarming press of rotting flesh.

The sound of their moans was irksome from this distance. He could imagine the sound inside the plane.

There was no way it was taking off.

Even as they watched, the pilot tried to turn the wheels, spin around on the asphalt and clear a path.

All it did was get him stuck more, the engines revving as he applied more torque to get them going.

The suction whipped a body off the ground and splattered it through the spinning turbine.

Followed by another, and another until the engine locked up on gore and meat.

The whine of metal on metal as it sheared off inside the housing echoed off the side of the plane and flames erupted from the compromised motor.

It popped and exploded, shrapnel piercing the wing.

Fuel splattered out across the motor from the holes, and the wing erupted.

One second later the plane exploded in a massive detonation that knocked Sharp and his squad to the ground.

He scrambled to his knees and ducked as zombie pieces rained down around them, and then half bodies began falling.

A torso with one arm landed on Combine.

He screamed and batted it away, but the dead latched on his

arm and bit.

He screamed again as it bit down harder, gnawing at the sleeve of his fatigues.

Javi jammed a knife through its head.

"Move! Move out!" Sharp screamed and led them away from the carnage.

The blast had blown huge sections of the herd in their way.

The squad ran through a gauntlet of mutilated animated corpses as they dodged left and right to avoid them.

25

25

"Open the gate!"

The two metal walls cracked out to let the running group of soldier's back into the compound.

They collapsed on the curb under the worried watch of the guards.

"What happened?" one called down in a panic.

He kept glancing over his shoulder to the Z that ambled from between the houses toward the now closed gates.

There were a lot of them, so many he lost count.

His fingers clenched and unclenched on the handle of his rifle.

"Get Doc," Sharp ordered Javi.

His Sgt. ran toward the auditorium where the rest of the squad waited.

He ran back with Doc in tow and the medic started examining Combine.

It didn't take long.

"He's bit," he announced.

"We know that," Sharp snapped. "Can you do something?"

Combine huffed and gasped, but didn't talk. Large tears leaked from the corner of his eyes and spread tracks in the dirt on his black cheeks.

They called him Combine because he tried out for the NFL twice before going into the service after college.

His speed on the field was almost poetic, and several of his squad mates knew him by name from watching highlight reels on sports talk shows.

It was like having a celebrity in the squad.
  Quiet, reliable, and dedicated.

"Give him morphine," Sharp ordered.

Doc backed away.

"Our supplies are limited Cap," he said. "I don't want to waste it."

Combine snuffled a sob.
   Doc meant he didn't want to waste it on a dead man.

Sharp grabbed the medic by the straps and yanked him down close to Combine.

"Help him."

Doc shook his head and struggled to get loose.

"Can't."

Sharp let go of the man and watched him roll away.

"Damn it!" he screamed.

He pulled the knife from the sheath on his vest and put the tip against Combine's temple.

"I'm sorry," he said and slid it in.

He pulled out the blade and the rest of his men sat there, watching him.

He knew they would want him to do the same.

None of them wanted to turn Z.

He hoped they would take care of him if it happened, though he figured on eating a bullet if it did.

Save them the hard part.

But he hated it.

He hated killing his man, the second on this mission.

All to save one person.

Sharp glared at Pam.

"You better be worth it."

He stood up, sheathed his blade and stalked off toward the middle of the compound.

Javi gave orders to Bear and Specs to get Combine up and out of sight while they figured out the next step.

He moved over to stand next to Pam.

"Don't say anything," she said.

He was impressed she wasn't crying.

He sure felt like it.

"I'm not making excuses for him," Javi said. "I was wondering if he was right."

"So was I."

She followed after Sharp, but instead of chasing him down, she turned to the porch that lined the front of the auditorium and planted herself on the steps.

She needed to think up a plan because right now, what they were doing wasn't working.

26

Sharp rounded the corner of the building at the far end of the compound and contemplated pounding the wall.

Jacob or whoever had come up with the design had done a good job of ringing off several blocks of the small town and putting up steel walls.

There was only one way in and out, which meant he had privacy back here.

It's what he wanted.

He should have cried.

That would have given him some release and vented the pent-up emotions that were gurgling in his gut.

But he didn't.

He stared at the wall, stared at the houses, studied the wind in the treetops, higher here since the obstruction blocked and changed the flow of the breeze.

He used a meditation technique they taught in training, practicing breathing in and out on a four count and let it wash a calm over him.

No plan ever survived contact with the enemy, which is why the training emphasized thinking on your feet so much.

A smile cracked his lips as he remembered a line from one of his favorite movies with Clint Eastwood.

"Improvise. Overcome. Adapt."

He wasn't a Marine but damn he could use their adage.

The Marine's had to come up with it because they were so often underfunded, outnumbered and facing overwhelming odds.

Yet time and again they came out on top and stuck it to the enemy.

Sharp wished he had a contingent of Marines under his command right now, or one good DI to smack him upside the head and ask him if he needed a wham-bulance.

They were trapped.

They were surrounded by zombies in the wasteland of the middle.

They had no intelligence about the threat, what survived or who.

So, as he figured it, they had two options.

They could wait and die.

Or they could take action.

He wasn't quite sure what the action was, but he had an idea.

The glimmer of one at least.

It would be an improvise for damn sure.

He wasn't certain if they could overcome with it though.

Sharp sighed.

He took a long deep breath and turned to go find Pam and Jacob.

27

27

"I have an idea," he said.

"So do I."

Sharp nodded.

He didn't plan to apologize to her and he was slightly impressed that she didn't ask for one.

Instead he found her sitting on the steps to the auditorium and thinking of the next thing to do.

"You first," he instructed.

"They thought your plane was lost, right Captain?"

"They sent a plane."

"I meant they thought you were lost when you parachuted in. Then you contacted them and they lost the plane. Do you really think they're going to send another?"

"It's your father," he waved her off. "You tell me."

"I think that he did the best he could, but they don't know what's out here. I don't think another plane is coming."

He glanced around at the compound.

"So what? You want to stay here and pioneer it?"

"No."

"Try to contact NYC?"

"No."

"Then what Ma'am?"

"I want to take these people to California."

"You just said they won't send another plane."

"Then we'll drive them."

Sharp snickered.

"Ma'am?"

"Could you stop calling me ma'am?" Pam huffed. "It's Pam. Ms. Ballantine if you can't manage that."

"Pam," he tried it on for size to see how it fit on his tongue and found he liked the way it felt.

"Why don't you tell me what you're thinking?"

"I think we need to get a caravan of buses or trucks and drive these people to the wall. It's only fifteen hundred miles."

Sharp looked away from her and stared at the wall to the West, as if he could see through it and to the horizon.

"Fifteen hundred miles that we don't know anything about."

"They won't come get us," she pouted. "I don't want anyone else to die trying."

"We don't have buses."

"We can find them."

"Fuel."

"We'll pick it up along the way. I'm not saying it's going to be easy."

"Food."

"They're running low on stores here. If we stayed, we would have to scavenge anyway. We can do it on the move."

Sharp shook his head.

"It's too risky."

"Staying here is risky Captain."

"My friends call me Sharp."

"Am I your friend?"

He stared into her eyes then and wondered.

This was the daughter of one of the most powerful men on the Council.

She had learned at the feet of her father. It was going to be tough to tell her no.

When he saw her eyes, he knew that it wouldn't be tough at all. Impossible was the word that came to mind.

"I'd like us to be friends," he said. "We'll need to be if we're going to pull this off."

That made her smile.

He liked how it looked on her cheeks.

"But it would be better for you and my squad to make the trip. Scout the lay of the land, get you home. Then we can decide to send a plane or bus back to get everyone else."

"No."

"No?"

"No. You dragged me out of here last time against my will and you saw how that worked out."

"You caused the zombie herd plane crash?"

She gave him a sad smile.

"These people are dying. We don't know how long they have left. Food is low. Morale is low. My father always told me people need hope. Hope for something better. If you give them that something, that vision of something, then they can move mountains. They have. Look at all we've done in the past, what we've overcome."

"And you'll give that to them?"

Maybe she would.

Her little speech had inspired him, moved him. He had a little hope.

Maybe she could make that spark up in the townspeople.

If that was all they needed, just something to work toward and aspire too, then he and his men would protect them.

Teach them to protect themselves.

He blew a long breath through his lips.

"Have you talked it over with Jacob?"

She shook her head.

"I wanted you on board first."

Smart, he thought.

She knew she could talk him into it, and if he agreed, then the leader of the community might buy it.

It beat waiting to die and was in line with what he had been thinking to share with her.

She just had to lay out the facts in a way he would understand.

He went with her so she could.

28

28

They found Jacob and shared the idea with him.

"You should just go on your own," he told her after she explained it.

Sharp almost spoke up to say he agreed, but held his tongue as Pam shook her head.

"You're starving," she ticked off her the tips of her fingers.

"You're going to have to hunt for food and scavenge. Your people are divided. If you stay out here, you're going to die."

Jacob hung his head and let her words wash over him.

They weren't new thoughts.

He had spent many nights thinking the same thing.

It was a matter of time, and he wasn't sure if he could watch his constituents starve to death.

"We might starve," he agreed. "Or we might find enough to keep going. But out there, we don't know what to expect. In here, some of us might die. But out there, some of us will die."

He glared at her then, not full of blame, but full of anger at her making him make the choice.

"If I talk us all into going, can you guarantee our safety?"

"Can you do the same if you stay?" she said. "These people, your people, need you to lead them across the desert."

"Do I look like fucking Moses to you Pam?"

"Watch your language," Sharp snapped.

"Sorry Captain, but what the fuck are you going to do about it?"

Sharp pulled his sidearm and clicked the safety off.

"Whoa, whoa Captain," Pam moved between the solider and the politician. "Don't you think that's a bit extreme?"

Sharp raised his pistol and fired.

Jacob flinched and collapsed on the ground.

"Jesus!" he screamed.

Pam covered her ears and stared at the soldier, a tiny trickle of smoke lifting out of the barrel of his gun and trailing across his face.

"You shot him?"

"No," the Captain corrected. "I shot a zombie."

He indicated a point past the mewling politico and Pam stared.

One of the hippies, a girl she had never met lay sprawled on the road.

Her gray skin was pasty, and even from here Pam could see two long jagged lines down her wrists.

Suicide.

Damn it, she shuddered.

Didn't these people realize how stupid suicide was inside the compound.

Did they even know how Z were made?

Where they came from?

Surely no one left alive was that stupid.

Killing yourself was selfish, but doing it now
    was almost murder.

A dead body turned Z and could kill or infect dozens more.

It was a biological time bomb, and she hated it.

Jacob picked himself up off the ground and ran a finger across his left ear.

"I felt it!" he shouted. "I felt the bullet whiz my ear."

Sharp shook his head.

"You heard it, yeah."

"See Jacob," Pam pointed. "You can't stay here. I don't want you to stay here."

"We were fine until you came along."

"Starving. Political dissent. You were one missed meal away from being Zombie food."

"Captain," Pam chided.

But she agreed with him.

So, did Jacob, even if he wouldn't put voice to the words.

"The walls you built are strong," she said to him. "You did a good job holding out until help arrived. This is help. We are your help."

Jacob shook his head.

"You're asking me to lose more people."

"I'm asking you to save as many as you can."

She let him think about that.

Pam could outline all the scenarios where staying here went wrong, but she suspected that those visions haunted his dreams at night, and maybe took up more than a few of his waking hours.

He could respond with all the things that could go wrong on a trip to the West.

This caravan was ill conceived, and ill outfitted for a long journey.

But until they found communications, it was the only way to reach help.

Her father would know what to do.

He would bully everyone onto the buses, send out a scout party for fuel and food, maybe more than one scout party to determine which way was most clear.

But he wasn't here. She was.

"You're coming with us," she told him. "We'll meet with your people tonight and come up with a plan."

"We're not. We can't."

Sharp put his hand on the weapon at his hip and waited.

Pam gave him a slight shake of her head to warn him off. She moved to sit beside Jacob on the porch.

"I know it's a lot to take in," she reached a tentative hand and placed it on his shoulder.

"I show up, you learn there's more out there but no one is coming to save you. Then these guys show up. You've lost people."

Jacob put his face in his hands and sighed.

"I'm responsible for their safety," he said through his fingers. "I can't guarantee that out there."

Pam looked at the dead hippie body up the street.
   He noticed and followed her gaze.

"You can't guarantee that in here either."

29

29

"It's not going to be safe out there boys."

Mickey moved around the narrow confines of a long room with racks on both walls.

There were hundreds of rifles, shotguns and pistols lining the space.

"I'm sure we'll find out first hand just how dangerous it is," he passed out weapons to the eight men in the room with him.

They looked hard, dirty, roughhewn features with stone expressions that watched him as he explained their mission.

"We're going in a little caravan across the country and I ain't afraid to tell you, this ain't no vacation."

He selected a Vietnam Era M-16 and checked the action on it, dusted the magazine on his leg.

"But there's rewards waiting when we come back."

"You told us hard work was its own reward," one of the men said in a gravel laced voice.

He was as wide as he was tall, a solid slap of beef in a leather duster with squinty eyes and a lump of a nose.

He told everyone his name was Murdock, and had said that lie for so long that he even believed it himself.

But Murdock was the name of the first man he killed back when he lived in Boston and worked for another Irish man.

There had been dozens since, each action building on his reputation, a tale that landed him in Los Angeles and under the tutelage of young Mickey.

Then the zombies.

He didn't count them on his mental kill list, but there were hundreds he could account for, including a woman who said she loved him.

Mickey smiled at him.

"Murdock," he picked up a burnished .45 off the bench and passed it to him. "If I were to tell you that our ship has come in, would you plaster a smile on your pretty face."

"I don't know Mickey, I get seasick sometimes."

"That's the spirt. Boys, what we have in front of us is a genuine opportunity where our actions earn recognition."

"I've done plenty that people recognize."

"I know you have Murdock and that's why I need your skills with me. We're going to be a couple of knights riding to rescue a lady in distress."

"You lost me."

"We've got us a mission boys. The big man himself is sending us on a joy ride to rescue his daughter and when we get back with her, he's giving us the keys to the kingdom."

He let that sink in while he slid magazines into an ammo pouch and slung it over his shoulder.

"You're saying we're going out there?"

"Over the wall."

"Out there with the zombies?"

"Yeah Murdock there's zombies out there. There's also a treasure in the form of Ballantine's daughter. We save her and we're set for life."

Murdock mulled it over in his head.

His mind was as lumpy as his features from a few knocks on it.

"But aren't all the zombies out there?"

Mickey stopped loading up his pouch.

"You're afraid of some walking dead people?"

Murdock shrugged.

"Afraid ain't the right word Mickey. Dead people are supposed to stay dead. We got most of the ones on this side of the wall, but out there? What are they? Millions of them."

"Yeah, probably," Mickey finished up one pouch and threw it into the arms of one of his men.

He started on another.

"But we're smarter than the Z's boys. And we've got each other. I looked at a map and it's a two-day drive to where she might be, and a two-day drive back. Add an extra day or two for trouble on a just in case basis and you're looking at a week to do this rescue."

"A million zombies in a week." Murdock grumbled.

Mickey glared at him, then set his face in a determined grin.

"We're not going to find all the zombies. In fact, we're going to move so fast we blow right past most of them. We're just going to pop out, grab her safe, and pop back in."

"That easy."

"It's simple. Not easy. We keep it simple, we watch each other's backs and we stay safe."

"I don't like it."

Murdock glanced around at the other men.

A couple nodded their heads in a show of support.

"You don't have to like it," Mickey stopped loading a ruck and faced the wide man who worked for him.

"What's the reward?"

There it was.

Mickey knew the man was loyal so long as the police weren't involved.

But this whole act was an angle for them to find out what waited for them when they returned.

Murdock just wanted a larger slice of the pie and he wanted to know what flavor he was getting.

Mickey took a step closer and said in a low voice.

"You're looking at the next member of the Council Murdock. You want to be on that side?"

Murdock let a large smile break across his wide face.

"Council huh?"

"That's right."

"Why didn't you just say so?" he turned to the other men in the group. "Those are the keys to the kingdom. We can fight a few zombies for that."

The men agreed, and they pitched in to finish kitting up.

Mickey had two SUV's waiting to carry them to the wall and beyond. He had planned for Murdock to be in one, the man was a de facto leader in his organization.

But the little show in the storage room made him reconsider.

"Murdock," he said. "You're riding with me."

30

30

Jacob had three other townspeople with him and Sharp brought in Javi and Bear, but they could tell Pam was in charge.

She had assumed the role with practiced ease like some alpha over a pack, and the others allowed her to do it.

It was the dynamics of her personality, along with some intangible way she carried herself.

Confidence was part of it, but it was also decisiveness.

Jacob bet she had been called bossy a lot as a kid growing up, and chided himself for thinking it now.

Bossy boys were called natural born leaders, and that's just what Pam Ballantine was.

A natural born leader.

He let his eyes drift to Sharp.

The soldier watched Pam with hooded eyes, studying her while she moved.

He was a leader by rank, but his men seemed to respect him.

Jacob had heard that he killed two of them once they were bitten by the Z.

That took a certain kind of guts, and he wasn't sure if he had those.

He was a leader by default, and he knew it.

The people looked up to him because of his role on the City Council, and he assumed the mantle because they needed it.

It had worked so far. Or worked out, if he thought about it.

But he knew it couldn't last.

The two factions had been at each other's throats since he put up the fortress walls.

Each week was something new, and this last stunt by Mike

nearly sent him over the edge.

Maybe it was time to pass responsibility on to someone else.

Maybe it was to her.

"What we're proposing is a radical option," she said as she stared at the men in the room. "But the fact is we can't stay here."

She studied them and Sharp gave her a small nod.

It might not have been encouragement, but she'd take it as such.

"My plan," she said. "They're not coming for us. So we're going to them. We can't survive out here, not long term. But Los Angeles is only fifteen hundred miles away. I say we load up in buses and make the trip."

"We don't have buses," said Jacob.

"We get them," she explained. "We get the buses, get supplies and move West to safety."

"But will it be safe?"

The man next to Jacob had watery eyes and looked on the verge of crying.

His black hair was slicked back from a long forehead that gave his face a weasel like appearance.

"Hamilton," Jacob introduced him.

"Ham," the man offered like it was a treat to call him by a nickname. "We're safe behind the walls."

"Captain," Pam glanced at Sharp.

"Your food stores are too low," he said. "Even if you go on half rations, you won't last the winter. Anyone dies in here, you're susceptible to Z attack inside the walls. That's going to take constant vigilance."

"We're doing that now."

"It's going to get worse as you get hungry," he explained. "You're asking these people to watch their children starve."

Jacob bowed his head.

"We could make it through the winter, scavenge and plant crops."

"Anything you plant won't be ready until summer, or end of summer," said Pam. "Can you last that long."

The three city men stuck their heads together to confer.

There was a little argument in their murmurs, but in the end Jacob shook his head.

"We can't last," he agreed.

"But going across the country," Ham said. "How do we know that's much better?"

"It's a chance. A fighting chance."

It was a tough choice she placed before them and she knew it.

"Choose to stay and everyone could die. Or the community would break down, the zombies would take over and a bunch of people would be out on their own."

She caught Jacob's eye and held it.

"But if we go out as a group, make the journey together, we can help each other. We can watch your backs, and you can watch ours. I don't know what's out there, but I know what's waiting at the end. Safety. Safer than here. A chance to rebuild."

Hamilton looked at Jacob.

"If the zombies got in, what would we do?"

It was a question they had asked before, but never had a good enough answer.

Jacob could see how Pam laid it out, and there was a chance things could go down like that.

People weren't rational, especially if they were starving and scared.

"How long would we be out there?" he asked.

She looked at Sharp.

"Fifteen hundred miles. No driving at night because we don't know what we'll encounter. Four hundred miles a day, maybe more, maybe less, so plan on five days."

"We have food enough for that long," said Jacob.

"Then we just need buses, or trucks to transport people."

"Will school buses work?"

The third man spoke up.

Everyone in the room turned to him.

"I'm Turner," he introduced himself. "I worked at the bus factory on the other side of town."

"There's a bus factory here?" Javi scoffed.

"It's not really in this town, more like a suburb, and we only did the finishing work for the school. But we called it the factory. The buses should still be there."

Sharp glanced at Pam.

"We can make an excursion to check, get a count."

"I don't want to lose any more people on this," she said and turned to Jacob.

"We need to find mechanics, anyone who can drive a bus. Load them up, make one trip and caravan them back here."

Jacob nodded, playing with the logistics in his head.

"While that group is gone," Pam continued. "The rest of the group packs in supplies and gear. When the buses arrive, we load up and ship out."

Jacob held up his hands.

"This is all moving too fast. It's not like we're starving now. We're safe. We can stay here for a week or so, then get the buses and take our time."

"We don't have a week," Sharp said. "We're moving fast. The longer we stay, the more people we could lose. There are people back in Cali who are waiting for us, who are worried about us."

"It's just, we're safe now."

"For how long?" Pam asked. "I've been here two days and you've had a revolt at the gate and a suicide. That's just what I've seen. You have a powder keg here, and the fuse is lit. It's just a matter of time before it goes wrong again, and when it does, you might not be able to contain it."

"We won't be here to stop another attempt to throw open the gates to zombie neighbors," said Javi.

"If you declare the move, you're giving people hope. You're giving them a vision to strive for and something to work to. They will rally behind you," she told Jacob.

He shook his head.

"They wouldn't rally behind me," he sighed. "If that were the case, it would have happened already. They wouldn't listen to me about the gate, about anything really."

"They have to," said Pam. "They need something to believe in."

"You. They need to believe in you."

She blinked.

"You're the one that's going to rally them," Jacob explained. "You're from the outside. You brought in outside protectors, soldiers to help you. That's what they see, that's what they believe. You can rally them to go West to safety."

Pam sat back in her seat and thought about it.

Maybe Jacob was right.

Maybe she was the catalyst to rally the people, and get them moving.

And get them moving fast.

The powder keg comment had just flowed out of her thoughts as she was talking to him, but now she could see that Hamilton, or Ham as he called himself was a sympathizer to the tie dye crowd.

She would have to win him over, but once the decision was made, she would work to sway him.

"Should we call a vote?" she asked.

"There's no vote. It's been decided," Sharp stood and his soldiers snapped to attention with him.

"You," he pointed to Turner. "You're taking us to the bus depot. Jacob, find us a mechanic and drivers. We move out in one hour."

31

31

Javi caught Sharp's eye as the meeting broke up.

Jacob and Hamm went to gather the rest of the survivors in the auditorium to lay out the plan with Pam.

Turner waited for the soldiers by the door.

"Hold back a sec, Sir."

"What is it?"

"Only hard men can survive out there. This is a bad idea Captain."

"I know it Javi."

"Then let's just grab this bitch and vamoose. "

Sharp thought about it.

Not for the first time.

Their mission was to save and retrieve one woman, not a town.

But she wouldn't go without a fight and it would be a long trip back home.

Forcing her to go would make that a hard trip and fighting Z would be tough enough without fighting each other.

"She's got the ball," he said to his Sgt. "She makes the call."

"You ready to lose more of us doing that Sir?"

Sharp grit his teeth and flexed a fist. Then he huffed through his nose and let it out.

"It's our job. We fight Z to protect people. It didn't stop when the wall went up, we just got distracted staying safe. Is this a bad idea? Yeah, maybe. But our mission is to protect those people and get that woman back to LA safe. You got a problem with that?"

He asked in a soft voice, but it still carried an edge to it.

Javi shook his head.

"I'm with you Cap. I just want to make sure your head is screwed on straight."

"I know the stakes Javi. I know what we're up against and what we have to lose."

They glanced through the doorway as Jess sauntered by on her way to the auditorium.

"I'm going to keep reminding you."

Sharp gave his Sgt. a grin.

"I don't want it any other way."

He left Javi to gather the rest of the men for the meeting in the auditorium. As he made his way up the stairs, Pam was waiting for him.

"You all right?"

He nodded.

"Yes Ma'am."

"Call me Pam," she said.

"I can't do that. We've got to get you a nickname."

"My Dad calls me Pamcakes."

"Pamcakes?" he snickered. "That doesn't make you sound very tough."

"I don't know, I think it's disarming. People hear it and they think cute little moppet with pigtails."

"You don't wear pigtails?"

"Only by special request."

"I'll remember that."

"See that you do, Captain."

They shared a smile, but his devolved into the semi-permanent frown that creased the corners of his mouth.

"I've got another special request."

"So soon," she teased but sobered up when she saw that he was looking for a serious moment.

"Pigtails reminded me. Where are all the kids in this creepy town?"

She glanced around and tried to remember the assembly, the gathering at the gate.

"I haven't seen any."

"Neither have I. I put SPECS on it, but nothing yet."

"Do they have kids here?" she wondered aloud, not really expecting him to answer.

Where were all the children?
   "No sign of kids either. You would think in a town this size, with this population that some of them would have children. They've been here a year, right?"

She nodded.

"In a year, no one's gotten pregnant? No new kids being born?"

A line creased the fine skin between her manicured eyebrows.

Even in New York the survivors were having babies.

The refugee camps were full of squalling and crying infants.

There was even protocol for it, a team of people on hand for complications in case of stillbirth, or the mom dying in childbirth.

It was rare, but had happened.

The team was there to make sure that neither came back Z or spread the infection.
   Would they have that same practice in the compound?

"I'll ask Jacob."

She said it to comfort the Captain, but he did not look swayed.

He looked like a man who didn't trust easily, and who thought asking Jacob might not be the answer.

She was glad he didn't say anything though.

That made her feel like he trusted her, or trusted that she would get to the bottom of it and report back to him.

"I'll get the answer," she assured him. "And I'll report back to you ASAP."

His frown didn't disappear, but it did soften a little to the hard line she had seen permanently etched on his face, like a scar on granite.

"You ready to set this thing in motion?"

She shifted her neck, stretching the muscles first one way, then the next.

He watched her put on a game face, roll her shoulders, like she was getting ready for a fight.

It was something he had done himself on many occasions. Stay loose. Stay ready.

"Let's get this started."

He followed her through the open doors.

Thank you for taking the time to read. If you enjoyed it, please consider telling your friends or posting a short review. Word of mouth is an author's best friend and much appreciated. Thank you. Chris.

www.ingramcontent.com/pod-product-compliance
Lightning Source LLC
Chambersburg PA
CBHW031624170726
47990CB00017B/359